Pineapple Upside Down Murder

Pineapple Upside Down Murder

Jodi Rath

Published by MYS ED llc

PO Box 349

Carroll, OH 43112

First Printing, November 23, 2018

https://www.jodirath.com

Leavensport, Ohio

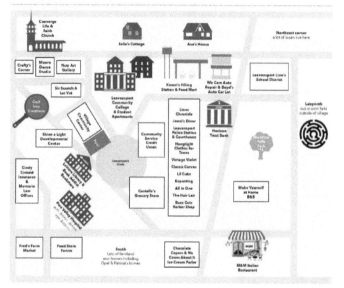

Converge Life & Faith Church

Julia's Cottage

Ava's House

Northeast corner
a lot of locals live here

Crafty's Corner

Moore Dance Studio

Nua Art Gallery

Leavensport Lion's School District

Sir Scratch A Lot Vet

Kwani's Filling Station & Food Mart

We Care Auto Repair & Boyd's Auto Car Lot

Cast Iron Creations

Labyrinth
out in corn field outside of village

Shine a Light Developmental Center

Village Community Center

Leavensport Community College & Student Apartments

Community Service Credit Union

Lions Chronicle

Jenni's Diner

Leavensport Police Station & Courthouse

Horizon Trust Bank

Leavensport Circle

Cindy Cincaid Insurance & Mercurio Law Offices

Leavensport Book Nook & Bindery

Vintage Violet

Classic Curves

Lil Cubs

Exposting

Make Yourself at Home B&B

Pine Valley Homes

Costello's Grocery Store

All In One

The Hair Lair

Buzz Cutz Barber Shop

Fred's Farm Market

Food Store Forum

South
Lots of farmland and homes including Opal & Patricia's homes

Chocolate Capers & No Cones About It Ice Cream Parlor

M&M Italian Restaurant

"The ultimate mystery is one's own self." –
Sammy Davis Jr.

Dedication

It is with a joyful and happy heart that I have an opportunity to write a dedication page. Without the following people, I would not be writing this page after having written a book. I'd like to give a shout-out to Sisters in Crime and the AMAZING Guppy group; I could not ever ask for a more wonderful group of people to learn from and share experiences with. I have to thank the wonderful women in my life: Rebecca Grubb, who has been with me since day one of this journey into this story and has been relentless about keeping me focused. Also, I have to thank Mary Ann Ware, who has cheered me on and supported me when I felt like I was not going to make it. Rosie Walton, my mom, what can I possibly say? You have inspired me my entire life. I have watched the strong, independent woman you are and aimed to be just like you. Evelyn Walton, my grandma, who unknowingly gave me the idea to write this series when she gave me her seventy-year-old cast iron skillet for Christmas. She told me the only thing she ever made in it was pineapple upside down cake and I needed to continue to do the same. I will, Grandma, I promise. I have to thank my editor, Lourdes Venard, who gave me incredible advice and who put up with me emailing her back and forth with what seemed like a million questions. You are my rock! Karen Phillips, who designed the cover, did a fabulous job in bringing Jolie to life. Lastly, I have to thank my husband, Mike Rath, and our eight cats ...my family. They have all been very patient with me as I type away. They have listened to my gripes and let me read to them and talk through scenes. If

I didn't have the support of my family, I would be nothing. You are the ones who make me everything. I love you all!

Last BUT NOT LEAST, I want to thank each and every one of you who purchased this book. I am so humbled that you would spend your hard-earned money on something I created. I feel so much gratitude for the kindness and support that I received from all of you! My hope is that you love and enjoy reading this book as much as I have loved and enjoyed writing it.

Hugs and Love,

Chapter One

I've always found *every* part of my life to be both beautiful and ugly at the same time. The next few weeks would not prove to be any different.

I knew my grandma's secret recipe for pineapple upside down cake by heart; it didn't stop my need to have the family recipe next to me when I made it. Now, like the cake, my entire world had turned upside down.

As I sat, I bent over and put my hands on my ears and laid my head in my lap, rocking slightly.

"Hey, Jolie, breathe. Look at me, please," Ava said with a concerned look on her face. Ava had been my best friend since we were in diapers, and she knew how I was when I was overwhelmed. She grabbed my hands and pushed me upright.

I was taking deep breaths, trying to calm my nerves. "I ...can't . . ." I was trembling and my long breaths turned choppy.

"We will find them. I promise." Ava gave me a big hug, thwarting my attempts to go internal. Ava always smelled of coconuts, and I caught a whiff as we embraced.

Ava and I had started a business a year ago

called Cast Iron Creations. The two of us decided to split the business fifty-fifty, with Ava running the front of the store and the finances, while I focused on the back of the shop, doing the cooking, baking, and shopping. Both of us pitched in with advertising, and I helped with the money occasionally. This was perfect because Ava was more of the social sort while I was more shy and comfortable working on my own.

The business was founded on my family's secret cast iron skillet recipes, which had been passed down for ages. My great-grandfather had carved out a wooden recipe box for the treasured recipes. On the bottom of the box, my great-grandma, grandma, mom, and now I have carved our names out. I spent my childhood with close friends Ava, Betsy, and Lydia pretending to cook in my grandma's kitchen in the cast iron skillets. Grandma's best friend, Ellie Siler, had been a big influence in my life.

I was hyperventilating because the Tucker family recipes had been stolen. Being a bit claustrophobic, especially in crisis mode, I slightly shoved Ava away from me as tears dropped off my cheeks.

"Hey, it will be okay. We need to pull ourselves together to figure out what happened," Ava said with a confidence I was not feeling at the moment. She pushed a thick, black ringlet behind her ear as she straightened her stance.

"You're right; I'm sorry," I said, standing and rubbing my hands against my apron. I was just getting ready to make my Grandma Opal's famous pineapple upside down cake. I always pulled the family recipes out when I baked; it was my routine. I kept the recipe box hidden in a false tile in our kitchen. When we bought the restaurant, I had wanted turquoise tile along the wall with the sink and oven; it reminded me of the ocean and helped make the kitchen a cheerful place to work. Ava's girlfriend, Delilah, Leavensport's resident artist, had made the false tile. But this morning, when I went to grab the box, it was gone.

"Listen, I know this is serious, but you know most of those recipes by heart, right?" Ava asked.

"I mean, yeah, I do, but I have my routine. Plus, I'm not sure I can live with myself if I'm the one who loses our family heritage. What will my mom and grandma say?" I wailed, on the verge of a full-blown outburst.

"Girl, stop, just stop for a minute. Everyone is always telling you that you are too hard on yourself! Stop trying to be perfect for once. Now, slow down, when was the last time you used them?"

"Yesterday was the last time I saw them, when I was making the cast iron steak special. I put them away at closing time," I said.

Ava rubbed her chin in thought. "So, you hid them last night, before we closed and locked up. It's 11 A.M. now, so someone had to have broken in overnight. Is there—" Ava stopped in mid-thought as Roxi walked through the kitchen toward the back door.

"I'm sorry, it slowed down up front, and I thought I'd take some trash out before the lunch rush," Roxi, our part-time help, said as she realized she had walked in on something serious.

"It's fine, Roxi, go ahead. Don't worry; we're trying to figure out an explanation to a problem," Ava said as Roxi moved quickly by me. "Did Roxi know where you kept the recipes?" Ava said when Roxi was no longer in earshot.

"Not that I know of, she rarely comes back to the kitchen during her shift," I said, trying to remember if I had ever taken the recipes out and had someone walk in on me. I had always worked to be careful so no one else knew where they were hidden.

"The first thing we need to do is write down all the recipes we remember," Ava said. "Then we can begin to figure out who took—" Ava was cut off as we both jolted at the sound of Roxi screaming from the alley.

Ava and I bolted through the back door. We found Roxi standing and shaking with a wild look in her eyes.

"What is it?" Ava bellowed, breathing heavily.

"It's Miss Siler," Roxi said, pointing a shaky finger at our dumpster. "I think she's dead."

Chapter Two

After phoning the police and calling an ambulance, Ava, Roxi, and I debated what to do next. "Should we check to see if there's a pulse?" I asked.

"What if she's not dead?" Ava said.

"Are you sure it's Ellie Siler, Roxi?" I asked.

"I'm not completely positive, but I think so. I jumped back quickly when I saw the body, but I saw one of her chocolate cat molds on the body," Roxi said. She began texting on her phone.

"Who are you texting?" I asked.

"My brother, Rex. He is supposed to pick me up shortly to take me to a class. I'm going to tell him I'm not going and I'll call him later," she said shakily.

Meanwhile, Ava tiptoed toward the dumpster as a man I'd never seen walked down the alley toward us.

"What are you doing?" the man barked at Ava.

Ava jumped back. "I'm just ...Who are you? I don't owe you an explanation!"

"I'm Detective Mick Meiser from Tri-City. And

you are?"

"I'm your worst nightmare Mr. Bigshot-thinks-he's-all-that-with-his-wavy-thick-locks-and-staring-down-at-me-like-some-big-city-know-it-all." Ava clipped her words in sync with moving her head.

"Again, who exactly are you?" I asked, trying to divert his attention from my defiant friend.

"Detective Meiser," he said again with an annoyed look while reaching into the dumpster. "She's dead. The chief will be here momentarily, and you three will need to stick around to answer some questions."

"Ava and I own this restaurant and Roxi works for us," I said, pointing out Ava and Roxi as I spoke.

"That's good to know. I didn't catch your name."

"I'm Jolie. Jolie Tucker. Miss Siler was my grandma's best friend. I can't believe she's gone," I said as the tears fell again.

"Have your grandma and Miss Siler had any altercations lately?" Detective Meiser asked, pulling a notebook from his back pocket.

"Hey, what's your problem? Do you think she's a suspect or something?" Ava snarled, getting right in the detective's face. Ava spent a lot of her time with my family growing up, and she was protective of all of us.

"Ma'am, you need to back up. I'm simply doing my job. I will need to speak to all of you at some point."

Meanwhile, Chief Tobias had pulled up.

"Detective," the chief said, nodding to Meiser as he walked to the dumpster. He slipped on a rubber glove to feel for a pulse.

"Chief to Dispatch."

"Dispatch to Chief, go ahead." The voice came through scratchily on the chief's radio.

"Code 11. We've got a 32 at 224 Cherry Drive in the alley behind Cast Iron Creations. Requesting coroner to scene. Go ahead, Dispatch," the chief said.

"Copy, Chief, 32 at 2-2-4 Cherry Drive alley behind Cast Iron Creations, read, go ahead."

"That's correct, Dispatch. Chief out."

"Dispatch out."

He seemed to be logging information from the scene. He looked inside and outside the dumpster, then bent down to look underneath it as he jotted down notes. Was he listing all the rotten produce surrounding the body? Ugh, a wave of nausea flew from my stomach to my throat as I compared the rotting produce to the decaying body of who I knew as Ellie Siler, the lady who helped raise me as a kid.

"A 32?" I asked. "That's a police code of some sort. Are you going to explain to us what that means?"

"Jolie, I know we go way back and are friends, but right now I have to put the job first. You are going to have to wait for an explanation," he said, then turned to yell at his officers, "Make sure you get the cautionary tape up while I'm inside the restaurant."

The chief jerked back to us. "I'll need you three to stand near the officers for a bit while I finish up here."

"Thirty-two means death," I stated.

"Sure, that's what it means," the chief said, turning away.

Teddy Tobias was all business, yet I still felt he had a softer touch, compared to the abrupt and cold Detective Meiser.

"We understand." I spoke for us all. "I don't know if this has anything to do with Miss Siler, but my family's cast iron recipes went missing today or last night."

As Chief Tobias wrote this down, Keith and Lydia walked up behind the caution tape. "Hey, Teddy, I wanted to check on the girls and make sure they are alright. Is it okay if I come through?" Keith asked as two deputies put hands up toward his chest.

At the sight of Keith, I caught myself trying to look casual while trying to get volume in my hair, using my fingers to scratch at the roots. Staring down at my rumpled pants, I went from hair to pants, trying to smooth them out.

Ava hip-bumped me with a knowing look.

Keith was a whole other complication in my life. I'd had a crush on him since junior high school. I tended to get nervous and fidgety whenever he was around. Keith and Teddy had been best friends as long as Ava and I had been. We all grew up together. Lydia and Keith seemed to be getting closer lately, and Lydia seemed jealous of Keith wanting to check on us. I figured she was here to check on her best friend, Betsy, who was Ellie's niece. I was right.

"I can't find Betsy; has anyone heard from her?" Lydia asked.

"He's okay, boys. But, Lydia, I'd like you to stay outside the tape for now, please," the chief said, "and Keith just stay further back away from the building while we finish processing everything."

Detective Meiser didn't look thrilled about Teddy's decision to let Keith inside the tape.

"Everyone is talking about this, Teddy. Jolie, Ava, Roxi, are you three okay?" he asked.

Before we could answer, Betsy appeared from out of nowhere and flew past the officers, moving quickly under the cautionary tape. The officers went to grab her, but the chief put a hand up to stop them. She tried to move toward the dumpster, but the chief intervened and grabbed her in his arms. Betsy desperately looked him in the eyes, "Teddy, is it true? Is she gone?"

"I'm sorry, Betsy, but your Aunt Ellie is dead," the chief said, looking down and unable to meet her eyes. Betsy burst into sobs, her face on the chief's shoulder as he held her tightly. She hugged him in return as he said, "I'm so sorry, Betsy; I'll do everything I can to figure this out. I promise."

Just then, Bradley, Leavensport's main reporter, came up behind the tape with his camera pointed at the chief and Betsy, snapping pictures of them and of the dumpster. Betsy seemed to be in a trance as the flash went off in the dark alley.

Lydia, in a fit of fury, went flying to Bradley. "You are a monster, a complete horror show!" she screeched and she reached out to grab the camera hanging around Bradley's neck. She yanked it hard and broke the strap while bringing Bradley to his knees in dismay. Ava, Roxi, and an officer jumped in to grab Lydia as she threw the camera down, stomped on it, and then kicked it against the wall, getting ready to move that foot to Bradley's head next.

"Back off and leave him alone," Roxi screamed at Lydia. She turned to Bradley, grabbing his hands.

"Are you okay?" Bradley seemed to ignore her.

"Whoa, as much as I think he had that coming, you don't want to get yourself in trouble," Ava said, grabbing Lydia and moving her away from a stunned Bradley. "Why don't you and Keith take Betsy home now?"

Lydia shook her head while glaring at Bradley.

The chief looked to Keith and signaled with a nod of his head toward Betsy. Keith picked up on his hint. "Betsy, let's allow the chief to do his job. Why don't you let me and Lydia drive you home or take you to your mom's house? Is that okay?"

Betsy nodded and Keith put an arm around her to lead her toward his car. "Wait," I said, running to Betsy. "Call us if you need anything," I whispered into her ear as I squeezed her.

"Anytime, too," Ava said, surrounding us in a hug.

"Thanks, I will," she sobbed.

Betsy ran into Lydia's arms as soon as she saw her, and the three moved out of the alley as Betsy kept trying to turn around to see what was happening.

"That's an expensive camera, and you will pay for that," Bradley yelled after Lydia.

"I think it's time you pack up and take off so we can finish up here," the chief said to Bradley while Ava gave him a satisfied look.

Bradley glared at Ava; there was no love lost between those two.

The three of us were waiting by the officers as we had been told when the ME showed up. Chief Tobias and the medical examiner were huddled over the dumpster discussing the situation for what seemed like two hours.

My head was spinning from the day's events. I couldn't believe Ellie was gone.

"Five, four, three, two, one. Ready or not, here I come!" I yelled, pulling my hands down from my eyes. "I can hear you giggling, Lydia."

Moving toward the giggling sound, I saw a large yellow caterpillar on the ground writhing from behind a bush and moving slowly toward a tree. The crunch of the leaves, combined with the giggles, gave Lydia away. "Gotcha!" I squealed.

Lydia rolled over and I helped her from the ground as she moved toward the cabin.

I caught a whiff of coconuts nearby. Moving toward the smell, I saw Ava's hot pink My Little Pony sweatshirt between a shrub and a tree. Ava was competitive, so she was not making a peep. I knew she was watching me. I turned away to circle around her. Closing in from behind, I was two long strides from tapping her.

"Run, Ava!" Ellie yelled as she scooped me up right before my attack.

"No fair," I cried out. "You cheated!"

Laughter filled the air as Ellie said, "You knew she was watching you; I saw you circle around. Nice strategy, Jo, you'll make a great dog catcher someday."

"I will not! I won't ever try to catch a dog. That's mean!" I stomped and crossed my arms.

"Oh, now, you all can play later. Your grandma wants you all in the cabin now."

"Why?"

"We are getting ready to start making the buckeyes. I'm sure you all would love some

*chocolate and peanut butter goodness." Ellie
swished her head around as Betsy moved out from
under a stump nearby; Keith and Teddy crawled
out from under a pile of leaves, and Bradley
jumped down from a tree.*

*"Gather around and grab hands, kiddos; it's off
to the cabin we go to make some buckeyes!" Ellie
said, leading the crew.*

Tears streamed down my face as I thought back
to Ellie scooping me up in her arms.

Thinking of the cabin in the woods brought back
that feeling of warmth that I typically experience in
our comfy little village, with its brick and stone
walks and colorful art on all the buildings. Right
now that was contrasted in this alley where I used
to feel safe with a feeling of dread.

My memories of Ellie and Grandma Opal
making homemade buckeyes at the cabin dissipated
as the chief walked over. "Okay, ladies, we will need
to shut your restaurant down for a week or so while
we investigate."

My thoughts still jumbled, I whispered in
confusion, "Investigate what?"

The chief cleared his throat. "We've found blunt
trauma on the back of Ellie's head. We have a
murder on our hands."

That feeling of trepidation was now turning into
horror.

Chapter Three

It was the middle of the night, and I couldn't sleep. My four cats were snuggled up to me in bed; they were my fur babies and it was proven in one way by my giving each of them a middle name. D.J. Lynn, my eighteen-year-old kitty, lay at my feet with Sammy Jr. Bobbi Jo liked to snuggle right up by my stomach. Lenny Lee liked to lie on the other side of me. Normally, I treasured my time with the kitties, but tonight the claustrophobia was setting in from the events of the day.

I slid up toward the headboard, trying not to wake my kitty crew. They seemed content in their spots as I twisted my body around them to get out of bed. I headed for my kitchen to bake the pineapple upside down cake I had planned for earlier in the day. The country décor with wood cabinets painted green and marble countertops made me want to cook nonstop. With the business closed, I had no one to bake for. But being in the kitchen always relaxed me. The first thing I did was write down the secret recipe for the cake. I mixed the ingredients as I thought about why all of this was happening. Ava and I had worked so hard this past year to get our business up and running. I had attended Leavensport Community College to get an associate's degree in culinary arts while Ava got her degree in business. We had been planning to open this restaurant since we were six years old. Of course, it was just for play as kids. Betsy, Lydia, Ava, and I would go into one of our grandparents' kitchens and take all the pots and pans out and pretend to run a restaurant. As we grew older, Ava and I continued to dream and discuss our restaurant. We would look through magazines and pick out stoves, refrigerators, flooring, tables, chairs, and murals for the walls. We spent endless hours decorating our pretend restaurant, conjuring up what now existed.

As the cake was baking, I sat on a stool at the counter to write down as many recipes as I could remember. How was I going to tell Grandma Opal that her best friend had been murdered behind my restaurant? Let alone that the family's legacy was gone? My stomach churned as the timer went off.

I got the plate ready. The pineapple upside down cake was almost ready to turn over, the scariest part of the process for me. Even though my mind had been wandering, I had to remember this was Grandma Opal's secret recipe and deserved my full attention. Grandma Opal had received this exact cast iron skillet over forty years ago as a wedding present. Since my grandfather's favorite dessert was pineapple upside down cake, Grandma Opal had only ever made this recipe in her cast iron skillet, which she passed down to me after my grandfather died. Generally, I kept the skillet at the restaurant, but last week I had brought it home with plans to do some maintenance on it. The skillet had begun to rust, and I wanted my grandma to come over to the house to help me get it cleaned up properly. I felt honored to carry on Grandma Opal's tradition of making the perfect cake in this priceless skillet. In fact, this had inspired my love affair of cooking with cast iron, and ultimately led to my starting Cast Iron Creations with Ava. Grandma Opal and Ellie Siler had created cast iron recipes years ago, with plans to open their own restaurant, but it never happened, and I had never understood why.

I proceeded to place cherries in the center of the gooey brown sugar baked into each pineapple ring. I cut myself a big chunk of cake and put the teakettle on the stove. While the water boiled, I leaned against the counter, looking out the window as darkness blanketed my backyard. I wasn't able to see the flower garden, trellis, and vegetable garden I maintained all summer. Now that it was fall, I'd have to think about the upcoming winter months and how best to protect it all. I was going through my mental list of vegetables I'd have to root up and which I could leave when I let out a small yelp as Bobbi Jo hopped up on the counter, rubbing her head against my hand.

"I know you want Mommy to get back in bed, don't ya?" I cooed at the small calico bobtail as she purred and rubbed her head even harder into the cusp of my hand.

We both jumped as someone knocked on my front door. "Who on earth could that be?" I asked as Lenny Lee came plopping down the steps. I switched on the porch light and peeked through the peephole. I quickly opened the door to find my Grandma Opal in tears.

"Grandma, what are you doing out so late? How did you know I was up?" I bombarded her with questions when instead I should have been holding her.

She let out a sorrowful sigh. "I heard about Ellie earlier this evening. I thought I was all cried out at home. I couldn't sleep, so I decided to drive around the village and when I came by your house, I saw some of your lights on and figured you were up. I'm sorry if I woke you, honey."

The copper antique teapot whistled. "Come on into the kitchen, and I'll make us some tea," I said.

My grandma was only five-foot tall and rotund, and she turned both feet out as she walked, making her waddle in the cutest way. I loved to watch her walk. Even though she was overweight from decades of bacon and eggs for breakfast, she moved fast. I turned the stove off to stop the noise and immediately turned around and grabbed her and hugged her tight. "I'm so sorry. I can't believe all this has happened," I said. I hadn't had the nerve to stop and see her after my interview with the detective and the chief. I was so worn out and it was late. I had talked myself into going straight home, hoping she wouldn't hear anything, but now I felt ashamed. Not to mention, I was terrified to tell her about the recipe box.

"I can't believe it either. I saw her earlier in the day at her chocolate shop. We were planning to get together next weekend to prepare for the Best Paws Campaign coming up next month. She had some ideas for making chocolate molds of cats and dogs for the auction. She had made two cats and two dogs so far." She smiled as she wadded a tissue in her hands.

"I forgot all about that. Too much has happened. I wondered why she was at our shop. She had one of her cat molds on her; I bet she was there to show me and Ava or to see if you were there."

I turned to get our tea made and cut another piece of cake for her as she said, "Jolie, what is this? Why are you rewriting all these recipes? The cast iron steak recipe is wrong too. You need to add the olive oil on the steak, rub it in with the salt and pepper, while the butter melts in the pan. You don't put the oil in the pan."

Oh boy. "Grandma, I'm afraid I have some more bad news," I said, placing the cake and tea in front of her in hopes it would help lessen the blow.

Grandma pushed the tea and cake back toward me. So much for softening the blow.

"Before Roxi found Ellie today, the recipe box went missing," I said.

"And just how does a box go missing? Did it run away?" she said with that stern look that made me wither.

"Of course not; what I meant to say is someone had to have stolen it. I know I didn't lose it!"

"Child, I cannot. I just can't. You let someone steal our family's recipes. The box your great-granddaddy made is gone too?"

"Um, well, yes. But I didn't let anyone steal it. I have no idea what happened. I went to get the box out and it was gone."

"Who knew where you kept it?" Grandma asked.

"Well, me, Ava, and Delilah. That's it."

"Wrong!" she said abruptly.

"What do you mean wrong?"

"I knew where you kept them too." She harrumphed.

"You have them?" I asked.

"Of course I don't have them. You need to make sure you have all your facts straight," she said as she pulled the cake and tea back to her and took a bite. Pointing to the cake, she said, "At least you remember this recipe; the cake's good."

I rolled my eyes. While I loved my grandma dearly, she could drive me a bit batty at times. When my mom, grandma, and I were all together, it typically ended in fireworks. We were all extremely stubborn, independent women who were too like-minded, except I was the quiet one. My family could definitely push my buttons, but I guess that makes sense, as they are the ones who installed them.

"Child, do not roll those pretty blue eyes at me. You need a perm," Grandma blurted out of nowhere. "Just because you lost our family's legacy and Ellie was murdered is no reason to go running around the village looking like a hag," she said bitingly.

I poked at my slice of cake, feeling two feet tall. "Yeah," I whispered in agreement.

"You know Ellie would tell you the exact same thing," she continued with tears welling up in her eyes.

I smiled slightly. She was right. Ellie and my grandma loved to pick on me together. Ellie always used to tease me when my perms were growing out. My blonde hair was normally fine and straight. I had no volume at all. Ava had beautiful naturally curly hair that I always admired, except she always straightened her hair. This turned into a typical argument between us. When we were eight, she talked me into getting a perm. I have to get them every three months to keep my hair looking decent. It's been five months, so I've been winging the hair thing and using a curling iron on the ends and pulling it back. Grandma saw it saggy and floppy in my eyes, since I had just been in bed. I think this was her way of scolding me for losing our family legacy.

"I know I do. I should have plenty of time this week, since the chief is closing down the shop to investigate Ellie's murder." I put my hand to my mouth quickly. I didn't mean to come off so blunt, even though I took after my grandma.

"Okay, well, there's nothing that can be done at this hour. We need to get some sleep. I'll just get out of your hair," Grandma said, avoiding the topic of Ellie.

"I was having trouble sleeping too. Why don't you stay with me tonight? Let's go up and get some sleep. I can get the other bed ready for you," I said, putting our dishes in the dishwasher.

We moved upstairs toward the bedrooms, and my grandma stopped me as I turned to go to the spare bedroom. "Wait, do you mind if I sleep with you in your bed? Do you think there is enough room?" she asked with tears in her eyes.

"Of course, it's a queen size. We may have to move some cats around, but I think we can all fit."

Chapter Four

The next morning, Ava came in while Grandma and I were having more cake and tea.

"I want some cake," she said, grabbing a plate and helping herself. She was wearing neon green tights and a paisley long shirt. Anyone would have seen her coming a mile away.

"And good morning to you too. I didn't even hear you come in," I snickered.

"I told her we should knock," Delilah said, standing at the door. She was more subdued in brown corduroy pants and a teal sweater.

"No worries, come on in and grab some cake and tea. Sorry you have to see us in our PJs," I said as Delilah came over and hugged me, then my grandma.

Ava and I had keys to each other's places and were next-door neighbors. We typically rode into work together daily; Ava drove, and I kept my bike at the shop, so I could ride around the village on errands when there was time.

Ava reached around Grandma's shoulder and

gave her a sturdy squeeze and kissed her on her head. "How are you doing, Mama Opal?" Ava had called my grandma this as long as she could talk. Delilah beamed with pride watching Ava in a tender moment.

"I'm here, baby girl," Grandma said softly, putting her hand on Ava's cheek. Bobbi Jo popped up on the table in between them and reached her paw out to tap Ava.

"What the . . ." Ava bellowed. Bobbi Jo and Ava had a long history of squabbles. It was rather entertaining to watch. "Girl, you better check yourself." Ava jerked her head back while Bobbi continued to reach for her. Ava gave in and picked her up reluctantly as Bobbi squirmed to be set free.

The kitchen door burst open and Aunt Fern and my mom, Patty, came bustling in, setting their large handbags on the counter and bickering about Aunt Fern's driving. Delilah moved back toward the corner of the kitchen. Very smart.

"You nearly killed us," my mom exclaimed wild-eyed.

"Overdramatic as always. Mom, do you remember when we were kids, and she used to cry when we rode our tricycles, and I'd bump into her?" Aunt Fern asked, facing Grandma Opal.

"Girls, you are too old to behave like children," Grandma scolded.

"Who made pineapple upside down cake?" Aunt Fern asked.

"Fernie, I'm cutting you and Patty a piece now; grab some tea," Ava said, winking at Delilah while hollering over the noise as Bobbi Jo finally freed herself and Ava turned to wash her hands.

"I want milk and sugar in mine," Aunt Fern said,

directing her comment to my mom. I caught a throbbing vein in mom's neck. She grinned at me.

At this point, Lenny Lee, D.J. Lynn, and Sammy Jr. came strutting into the kitchen to see what all the commotion was about. Sammy Jr. was the wariest of the four cats, so he hid under the table as he observed my family reunion. I wanted to be under the table with him right now. I understood Delilah's move to the corner.

Aunt Fern went nuts for Lenny Lee. She had four dogs, so she loved that Lenny had dog tendencies. Lenny was mistaken for a dog when found in a dumpster. The lady thought his paws looked like a puppy's so she called the dog pound. Aunt Fern had gone to the pound to pick out a new dog and saw Lenny. She fell in love and brought him to my house, demanding I take him.

She grabbed his toy mouse and threw it; he ran, retrieved it, and brought it right back to her as she said, "Good boy, that's Fernie's good boy."

Meanwhile, I caught my mom pulling Grandma into my living room. I'm sure she was checking on her after the shock of losing Ellie.

Ava took a sip of her tea and looked at me. "So, what are we going to do this week since the restaurant will be closed?"

"I was just thinking about that."

Aunt Fern had heard and turned around. "Why don't you run your business out of your kitchen, Jolie? Several of us will be working on the Best Paws Campaign for the adoption coming up in a few weeks. We will all be at the community center. I can talk to the mayor to see if we can order lunch and snacks for everyone from you."

"That would be wonderful, and I'm sure the

mayor will agree if *you* ask him," I said, waggling my eyebrows at her.

Ava gave her ornery grin and mimicked Aunt Fern. "Oh, Mr. Mayor, I would be eternally grateful if you'd help out my poor dear niece, Jolie, this week." Then she winked with her hands held up to her heart. Delilah giggled.

Aunt Fern got that stubborn bulldog look and shook her finger at us. "Just forget about it now. Try to do something nice for someone, and this is what you get!"

"Now, Fern, you behave and make sure you ask the mayor. Your family needs your help," Grandma Opal said, walking back to her stool and grabbing a forkful of cake. She paused before taking a bite and, with a twinkle in her eye, added, "And make sure you wear blue, since that's his favorite color."

Aunt Fern crossed her arms and changed the subject, asking, "Has anyone visited Betsy? How is she doing?"

"Ava and I saw her yesterday; she came running through the crime scene trying to get to Ellie, but Teddy caught her. It was horrible. I feel so bad for her. I don't know what to say," I said.

"Yeah, Keith showed up, and he took her home. That new detective wanted to keep her there for questioning, but she wasn't at the scene of the crime. That man has no manners," Ava said.

"New detective?" Aunt Fern questioned.

"Detective Meiser, he's from Tri-City; I'm guessing he's in town for a few weeks—hopefully," I said.

"Why do you say that?" Aunt Fern asked.

"Like Ava said, he's rude. Doesn't talk much."

"Your stepdad was reserved too," Mom said.

I jerked my head back like I'd been slapped. I didn't like comparing the detective to my stepdad, who I held on a pedestal.

"Wait, is he tall, with thick wavy brown hair, and big brown eyes, square, strong jaw?" Grandma Opal asked as Ava, Mom, Aunt Fern, and I stood mouths open, looking at her.

"Um ...yeah, Mama Opal, how'd you know?" Ava asked.

"I saw him at the credit union the other day; he was in front of me in line," she said.

"Well, I guess I should have known you are a stickler for details in a man's appearance since you seem to know the mayor's favorite color is blue," Aunt Fern said in payback to Grandma's dig at her and the mayor.

"He did have nice hair," I said, "unusually thick."

"Hmmm ...so, no more crush on Keith?" Ava asked.

"Oh shush, I just happen to notice anyone with thick hair. It's called hair envy," I said as I ran my fingers through my hair, trying to get some volume.

"Keith has nice hair too," Grandma said. She's always rooted for us. Ellie, on the other hand, never seemed to think Keith was good enough for me. Ellie told me once that Keith reminded her of my biological father—this was one possible reason why I feared relationships, not to mention messed up any chance I ever had with Keith.

"So, Aunt Fern, you are going to talk to the mayor about us cooking for the Best Paws volunteers this week, right?" I asked, changing the subject.

"Yeah, I'll take care of it."

"Great, thanks," I said, then added as an afterthought, "Grandma, did you ever tell Ellie where I kept the family recipes?"

"She knew you kept them in the kitchen of your shop, but I never told her about the tile. Why?"

"I don't know exactly. It's just strange that the recipes went missing and then Ellie was found behind our restaurant."

"What are you thinking?" Ava asked.

"I don't know yet, but I plan to visit Betsy this afternoon to see how she is doing." I intended to see if she could help me shed some light on this.

Chapter Five

Betsy lived inside the village near my house, which was located just outside of town. It was late fall, my favorite time of year, and the air was crisp and the leaves were changing colors. It was perfect weather to ride my bike to her house. But first, I wanted to ride by Cast Iron Creations, both to get a little more of a workout—I've always been one who has to exercise constantly to be able to eat what I want, not to mention I quickly put on weight—and to see our restaurant. I already missed it. Lord knows I could use it after the morning with my family.

A cool breeze blew through my hair as I walked to my bike rack to unlock Gertrude, the name I had given my bike. As I entered the village, I cycled down the layered brick art walk paths and slowed down, moving past the restaurant with the "Temporarily Closed for Death in the Family" sign we had made. I lowered my legs to the sidewalk, coming to a halt, and back-shuffled to the front window of the restaurant. Stepping off Gertrude, I leaned her on the wall of the shop and sat at the bench we put outside the door.

As I leaned my head back, I thought back to the day we opened the restaurant. Tears welled up in my eyes when I thought about prepping the front of the store with the Victorian cast iron table bases and glass tops, adding fresh flowers daily to each table. Delilah painted a beautiful mural of our village across one wall while the other wall had a cute bay window with a built-in bench and comfy cushions to sit on and read, relax, and sip some tea. Most of the Leavensport villagers frequented our restaurant, stopping in for baked goods and coffee or tea in the mornings, take-out daily specials for lunch, and dining dates or family gatherings for dinner. Ava and I prided ourselves in making it as homey as our village had felt our entire lives. Waves of fear rushed through me as I thought about Ellie's murder and how that would affect the business. Next, guilt blanketed my soul—why was I worrying about losing the business when Ellie was dead?

"Jolie?"

I was jerked out of my reverie to see Rex, Roxi's brother, standing over me. Rex was the quarterback for Tri-City's college football team. While Roxi had just finished high school and now was at the community college, Rex had received a scholarship at the big city college.

"Hey, Rex, how are you doing? I haven't seen you in a while. Are you okay? It's a little cool out here and you seem to be sweating."

"I'm okay. Sorry if I scared you." He held up a duffel bag. "I was just at the gym; that's why I'm sweating."

"I was lost in thought," I said, standing to give him a hug. He was a few years older than me, but we all knew each other around here. "What brings you back to town?"

"Roxi, she's been having some trouble with her college classes. She's taking a psychology class and I've already had to do that one, so I figured I'd come back and visit the family for a few days."

"Big brother duties, huh?"

"Yep," he said looking down as his phone vibrated. "Actually, duties call. This is Roxi texting me now. It was good to see you."

"You too, Rex, take care."

Yikes, I thought to myself, seeing the time on my watch. I hadn't realized how long I had been daydreaming. I needed to head toward Betsy's place.

I hopped back onto Gertrude and biked past the Moore Dance Studio, where colorful graffiti commissioned by the owner filled the walls on the outside. I looked to my left at the Nuu Art Gallery, where Delilah worked, with its red barn appearance. Next, I glanced to my right at Sir Scratch a Lot's veterinarian clinic, with its pastel-colored dog and cat paws that covered the old brick building.

I slowed again as I saw Lydia walk into the hospital with Bradley. The hospital only had three floors, since the population of our village was small, but the building fit in with the look of the rest of businesses. It was a warm shade of cream with dark brown wooden shutters around all the windows. Lydia and Betsy both worked as nurses at the hospital. I couldn't understand how Lydia and Bradley could have just had that drag-out fight in the alley and now they seemed like bosom buddies walking into the hospital.

I thought about that as I cycled through one of my favorite places—Leavensport Community

College Campus. The lawns were lush and green, and the plentiful trees were beginning to change with the season, showering red-orange, yellow, and bright green leaves on me as I rode. The brick buildings towered over the trees, making me think of all the wonderful books that filled them. My mind immediately flipped back to wondering what Bradley and Lydia would be talking about.

I continued riding for a few minutes more before arriving at Betsy's apartment near campus. I hopped off my bike and leaned it against Betsy's outer wall, looking longingly over at the Leavensport pool. It would be several months before I could again sunbathe the weekend afternoons away.

"Jolie, what's up?" Betsy said. I hadn't noticed she was sitting on her patio. Betsy took after her Aunt Ellie with her green thumb. Her patio was filled with pots of orange and rust-colored mums. There was a flower garden with looming lilies and oriental grass trimmed back to the exact right length for the tiny area.

"Sorry, Betsy, I decided to take a bike ride and was just looking at the pool, thinking about how quickly the seasons change."

"Yeah, that's so true," Betsy said. I could tell she had been crying by the swollen skin around her eyes. As I moved toward her, I noticed a box of tissues. Many of them were wadded up on the ground. I leaned over to hug her.

"I hope it's okay I dropped in on you; is your mom here?"

"No, Keith and Lydia took me to my mom's house yesterday, and I stayed a few hours. That was all I could handle. Mom and Aunt Ellie were close but not as close as I was to her. You know how she was always there for me when Mom and I butted heads over the years. She was our bridge, and now that she's not here I don't know what to do when Mom drives me nuts. Who do I go to?"

"You can come to Ava or me, Betsy. Really. You don't have to go through this alone," I grabbed her hand and squeezed it.

"I appreciate that. I feel bad not being there for my mom but . . ." She started crying again.

"You need to take care of yourself too," I finished for her as she nodded her head in agreement.

"You want to help? Be like Aunt Ellie and take my mind off this, please. She was always so good at taking my mind off my troubles."

"I don't have any chocolate on me."

Betsy laughed; it was great to see her smile momentarily. "Yes, you're right; chocolate was an easy way to my heart. You know I was thinking about leaving the hospital to take over Chocolate Capers for Aunt Ellie?"

"I had no idea. You've only been a nurse for a year, right?"

"Yeah, who knew? Honestly, I didn't like the job that much. Lydia is a way better nurse than me. I loved working with her, but to me it was just a job, not a calling. When Aunt Ellie said she was thinking about retiring, I asked her who would take over her chocolate shop. She said she had always hoped I would take over, but since I was a nurse, she wanted to sell the shop."

"I didn't know she was thinking of retiring. I wonder if my grandma knew."

Betsy had started sobbing again. "I'm not sure. I

had given it a lot of thought and decided I wanted to take over the business. I hadn't had a chance to tell her yet."

I grabbed her hand again, "I'm sorry; I'm doing a horrible job at taking your mind off it. Ellie would swat me on top of my head." That brought back another smile.

"She'd also be on you about it being time to get a perm."

"You don't need to tell me that. Grandma and I just had this conversation."

"Those two were relentless when it came to appearances," Betsy said with a giggle. "I'm sorry; I haven't offered you anything to drink. I made some fresh sun tea this morning. It reminded me of Aunt Ellie. Would you like some?"

"That sounds great, but why don't you let me go get us some? Ellie and Grandma would tell you to clean yourself up," I said, grinning at her.

"That they would." She laughed again.

Like the patio, Betsy's kitchen and living room held many potted plants in full bloom. It looked like she had some herbs growing in small pots by the window too. While I was making our glasses of tea, I looked for a spoon to stir some sugar into mine and noticed some of the dog and cat molds my grandma had mentioned last night. I picked up one in each hand. They were really cute, and it was a great idea to make chocolate cats and dogs for the auction. That was one of the many reasons I loved living in a small village. We all came together annually to do an auction to help the strays that ended up in town. Dr. Libby, the local vet at Sir Scratch a Lot, and her staff ran it, but most of the folks in town volunteered and helped out too. I was getting ready to put the molds back in the drawer when Lydia barged through the door.

"Why are you snooping around in Betsy's kitchen?" she said with a glare.

I was a little shocked by her rudeness. "Hi, Lydia, Betsy just ran back to the bathroom to clean up. I came by to see how she was doing and we decided to have a glass of tea. I was looking for a spoon so I could put some sugar in mine. Would you like a glass?"

"Here, let me get my own," she said, reaching into the next drawer and pulling out a spoon for me. "How is she doing?"

"She was crying when I got here, and she's been crying most of the time I've been here. I did get her to laugh a couple of times, though."

"Well, that's a good thing. I just can't believe that this happened. Ellie and I had our differences, but I'd never wish this on her."

"I always thought you and Ellie loved each other."

"Oh we did, at least she loved me when I was a kid, not so much as an adult." Lydia stared off into the distance.

I felt like a change of subject was needed. "Hey, I rode my bike over here and saw you and Bradley walking into the hospital together. Is everything alright?"

"Of course everything is alright. I work there, you know?"

That wasn't the answer I was hoping for.

"I just thought it was weird to see the two of you together after the scene in the alley yesterday," I pried.

"That's in the past," Lydia said.

"What's in the past?" Betsy said, grabbing her glass of tea as I held up the sugar; she shook her head no and we all moved back to the patio.

"Oh, nothing, it's just Jolie nosing around." Lydia grinned like it was a joke, even though her words stung a bit. "How are you?"

"About as well as can be expected. I don't want to talk about it right now. I just splashed some water on my face. So, why were you with Bradley?" Betsy asked.

"You heard that, huh?" Lydia said, eyeballing me. "Bradley wanted to apologize for the other day. I guess he's learned about the importance of family and keeping good relationships since he's had a falling out with Delilah," Lydia said, still glaring at me.

"Ava tried to tell Bradley she wasn't interested in him but he wouldn't listen," I said in her defense.

"I think she could have been more straightforward and told him she was interested in his sister instead," Lydia said, crossing her arms.

"Well, I would think that would be a difficult thing for Ava to do. It's not her fault Bradley fell for her and was so persistent. It wasn't like she was leading him on or anything. It seemed to me she was trying to spare his feelings," Betsy said.

Betsy's words got Lydia to back off. Ava had boyfriends when we were growing up, but she never took much interest in them. When we became teenagers, she came out to me first, then I went with her to tell her family. They were great; my family was great. Actually, the entire village had been great. No one knew Bradley had carried a crush for her for years. When he found out she was gay, he seemed to refuse to believe it and pulled all kinds of romantic stunts. That was one problem; the bigger problem was that Ava was in love with Bradley's sister, Delilah, and vice versa. This had caused a huge division between the three. The entire situation started toward the end of our senior year of high school and progressed as Ava and Delilah began dating, to Bradley's dismay. Last I heard, Bradley and Delilah weren't talking.

"I need to head out to the credit union," I said, wanting to get out of this conversation.

"Thanks so much for stopping by; you cheered me up," Betsy said.

"Yeah, thanks for watching out for Betsy," Lydia said, getting up to take my glass inside.

"Anytime, and I meant what I said earlier, Betsy, feel free to reach out to Ava or me if we can help with anything."

"She'll be fine, Jolie, but thanks," Lydia said.

Chapter Six

The village credit union looked like any other financial establishment, except there were bowls of chocolate sitting around the reception area, on the deposit counter, and on each teller's station with a picture of Ellie next to the chocolates. The village was rallying around Ellie's family and showing their support. While I was standing in line, I smiled at the familiar faces around me from the village and noticed a tall, dark-haired man who stood in line in front of me. I was trying to nonchalantly get a view of his profile to see if it was Detective Meiser when two tellers opened up at the same time. I walked up to my teller, who was Keith's sister, Denise, and asked if she had a deposit slip.

"Just depositing today then, Jolie?" Denise asked as she handed me a deposit slip under the clear protective window.

The man next to me glanced over at with large brown eyes that matched his thick brown locks, and I quickly looked down as a red blush crept to my cheeks. It was Detective Meiser. I looked back up to smile, but he looked away, so I responded to

Denise. "Um yep, how have you been?"

"Can't complain any because no one cares, right? We all have issues we carry around with us. Why are mine any more important than anyone else's?" Debbie noticeably tried to straighten her stance in bravery.

"Good point. That's a good perspective to take," I said, trying to catch another glance at the handsome Detective Meiser.

"Yeah, I'm reading some of the self-help books, since Darrell decided to look for greener pastures. Trying to be a good role model for my Jazmine."

"Good for you! If I can do anything to help, just let me know."

"You are such a dear! When are you and my brother going to go out on another date finally? That man needs to get his priorities in order," she said, too loudly for my liking.

I noticed that Detective Meiser looked over at her briefly.

"Um, I don't think that's going to happen. I thought he was seeing Lydia," I said in a whisper, hoping that would give Denise a hint.

"Lydia's always had a thing for Keith. You know that. I overheard her telling Keith that Miss Ellie had stage four cancer the other day. Odd that she would end up dead behind your restaurant." This time Denise did lean in closer to me and whisper.

"What?" I said in complete disbelief. "That can't be. I would know that. She would have told my grandma or Betsy would have told me," I said, trying to make sense out of this new information.

"Sounded like no one knew but Lydia. She was telling Keith that she was secretly treating her,"

Denise said.

"I just can't believe it," I said, stunned. I noticed a line growing and said, "I'm going to get out of your hair. You take care, Denise."

"You too, hun."

I was still in shock from the news as I slammed into Detective Meiser, who was standing at the station next to me, "Sorry, are you okay?" I asked.

"I'm fine; better keep your eyes open a bit more, huh?" he said rather sharply and hurried off before I had a chance to respond.

That was rude, I thought. Hopefully, this man was not going to be a regular in the village.

*

By now, I was running late. I still had to run home to pick up Bobbi Jo. She had an appointment with the vet. I had my Bluetooth earbuds in and was listening to music on my phone as I rode through the village. I stopped momentarily to dial Ava's number, then began biking again.

"Hey, girl, what's up?" Ava said.

"What are you doing right now?" I asked.

"Not much, just watching some stuff I had on the DVR," she said.

"I have to bring Bobbi Jo into Sir Scratch a Lot's, and I'm running late. I'm near the vet's office now. Do you think you could grab her and meet me here, please?" I added in the hopes this would work.

"Uh-uh, no way! You know she and I don't get along. You did this on purpose, didn't you?" she huffed.

"No, I did not do this on purpose, and it is ridiculous that you are saying you don't get along with my cat."

"You know that's not what I mean. She is absolutely nuts when you try to put her in that carrier. Last time, she scratched you all up and down your arms. Don't think I don't know what you are up to!"

"Ava, wear long sleeves. I didn't do this on purpose. I stopped to see Betsy and then had to run to the credit union. I found out some interesting information. If you bring Bobbi Jo here, I'll tell you," I prodded.

"You'd tell me anyway," she said unpersuaded.

"Come on; she's supposed to be here now. If I ride my bike home, then get her, then drive back, we are going to be so late," I pleaded.

"Oh, okay. Geesh! You are such a whiner! You are stayin' on this phone while I get her. If I'm doing this, then you will hear the pain I endure."

"Okay, I'm heading into the waiting room now. I'll stay on the line," I said as I walked into the brightly painted yellow room, which had brown cats and dogs stenciled all over the walls. Stacey was working up front and looked concerned when she didn't see Bobbi Jo with me. "I know I was running late; Ava is bringing her in right now. I'm sorry I'm late," I said.

"No worries, Dr. Libby is running a bit behind anyway," Stacey said.

"Are you kidding me?" Ava yelled.

I thought she was yelling at Bobbi Jo, so I said, "What is she doing?"

"Nothing, I just got the crate out, and I'm looking for her now. I was talking to you. First off, you pull this stunt on me, then you don't even bother to thank me, then I hear you apologizing to them and telling them I'm running late?" Ava said angrily.

"I did not say you were late! I said I was running late. Calm down!"

"I still have not heard a thank you," she grunted.

"Thank you," I said bitingly.

"You are lucky we go way back."

"I know." I softened my voice.

"Girl, I see you. Where are you going? No, I am not crawling under that bed. Bobbi Jo, get out here right now," Ava demanded.

"She's not going to come out; you need to force her out," I said.

"Got it."

"You got her already?"

"No, I just ran into your bathroom and grabbed your broom to force her out."

"Don't hurt her," I squealed.

"Do you want me to bring this cat of yours in or not?" Ava asked.

"Yes, in one piece and not hurt," I said.

"I'm hanging up now," Ava said.

"I thought I was supposed to stay on the phone. Go grab the treat bag in the cupboard over the refrigerator and shake it. That will get her out." I waited, taking a seat. "Did that work? Hello?" I wondered how long ago she had hung up.

I sat in the waiting room, thinking back to what Denise had told me about Ellie. The last few times I had seen Ellie she had been pale, and we were worried about her, but she told us she had caught a bug and was weak. Why wouldn't Lydia tell Betsy? I couldn't understand it. Oddly enough, my phone rang, and it was Betsy calling me.

"Hey, I was just thinking about you," I said.

"Hi, Jolie, do you have a minute? There's something I need to tell you," Betsy said.

Right then Delilah came out of a patient room with her schnauzer, Poptart. "Hi, how are you?" she asked.

I got up and hugged her and scratched Poptart on his gray head, pointing to the phone. She nodded in understanding.

"Hey, are you out? I hear someone. Don't worry; I'll give you a call later," Betsy said.

"Are you sure? Are you okay?" I asked.

"Yeah, it can wait. Bye."

I turned back to Delilah. "Sorry about that. I'm doing good; how are you?"

"I'm okay; I'm so sorry if Ava and I barged in the other day. She was worried about you, though. I know she was thrilled Opal was there, because she was worried about her too."

"Thanks, it's horrible. My grandma is beside herself. She's putting on a brave face, though."

"Yeah, your family is something else. I wish my family were as close as yours."

"That's nice of you to say. Although I could live without them barging into my house at all hours of the day. I hope you and Bradley will be able to iron out your differences," I said, not knowing exactly how to approach that tricky topic.

"I expect we'll work through it one way or another. Ava says she wants us to make up, but she's not always great at showing it when she's yelling at Bradley every time she sees him."

My mind went blank as I went twitchy from feeling awkward, so I changed the subject. "Speaking of Ava, she should be here any minute now. I was running a bit behind and asked if she would drive Bobbi Jo in for me."

Delilah gave me an amused grin. "Oh boy, she has a real distaste for that cat. She gets mad at me because I make fun of her. I can't help but think it's all a game." I was getting ready to respond when Ava came bounding into the office with a duffle bag that looked like a Tasmanian devil was inside it.

My eyes bulged out of my head as my heart leapt into my throat. "You better not have my cat in that bag," I said agitatedly.

Delilah took two steps back toward the kiddie play area in the waiting room and began fiddling with the Legos, trying to avoid the confrontation.

I took four big steps toward her, my arms held out to the bag.

Ava moved back with a hand up. "Oh, she's in the bag. She refused to get in the carrier. She took that tiny little body of hers and planted her paws against the sides and made the most horrendous screams I've ever heard. She scared me to death. So I grabbed the nearest bag and tossed her inside; it's all I could do." She glared at me, daring me to argue.

"I cannot believe you did this," I said, stomping the last few steps toward her to grab the bag with angry tears in my eyes.

Stacey stepped in. "Jolie, it looks like she has the bag partially unzipped and it looks like there are some holes in the bag. I'm sure Bobbi Jo is fine."

"Yeah, she and I don't get along, but I don't want to kill her. I've got her toy squirrel in there, and I made a few extra holes to make sure she can breathe. I've got her crate out in the car in case you want to put her in there before we head home. You take her; I'll go get the crate and put your bike on the rack." She hightailed it out of there. Ava normally was not afraid of me; it generally was the other way around, but she knew when she had taken it too far.

Stacey grabbed the bag from me. "I'm going to take her back to a room and get her weight, and we will start with cleaning out her ears. Why don't you take a minute to calm down? Then you can come back."

"Thanks," I said. As Stacey walked back and as an afterthought, I called out, "I'm sorry." She didn't even turn around, but just waved a hand in the air.

"Ava means well," Delilah said.

"I know, and I can't be that upset with her as I'm the one who called her last minute begging her to do me this favor," I said, shaking my head.

"She told me about what happened with Bradley at the scene the other day. I'm sorry he caused so much angst during a trying time," she said with tears in her eyes.

I'm sure it was difficult for her to be on the outs with her brother. "Lydia was the one who went ballistic. It was weird because that just happened and today I saw the two of them walking into the hospital all buddy-buddy."

"I wish I could tell you, but, as you know, he and I don't talk much anymore."

"Well, I hope you don't take offense from this, but did you ever tell Bradley about the secret tile where I keep my family's recipes?"

"No, I wouldn't tell anyone; I promise."

"I believe you. Did Ava tell you they are missing?"

"Yeah, I'm sorry all this is happening. I don't know how you are dealing with it all."

"Well, Betsy is the one who is going through a lot right now. I can handle having the restaurant shut down temporarily."

"I know, but what will you do if Ava moves?"

I stared at her dumbfounded.

"Uh, I need to learn when to keep my mouth shut. Gotta go," she said and sprinted with Poptart out of the office.

Chapter Seven

I was in the back patient room of the vet's waiting for Dr. Libby to bring Bobbi Jo back to me. The sterile scene numbed my mind momentarily, but then it began to whirl with the events of the last two days. I loved that I could be in the back of the kitchen in the quietude of cooking and baking and dreaming up new recipes or playing around with the family recipes of the past to make them more modern. I was so content in my life. It all changed on a dime. Now, I had to find out from someone else that my best friend was moving?

"This one is a pistol," Dr. Libby said, bouncing in and laughing with Bobbi Jo squirming and growling in her arms. She had her dog and cat scrubs on and was happy and perky as always.

"Yeah, Ava didn't help matters," I growled. I couldn't help but feel betrayed.

"She's fine, just spunky."

"Ava or Bobbi Jo?" I asked.

"Both," Dr. Libby belted out with her boisterous laugh. She had a way of making me feel more comfortable. It must be why she was always swamped. Animal lovers were drawn to her as much as the animals were. "I trimmed those claws before cleaning out her ears to save myself a lot of pain."

"Smart." Bobbi Jo had allergies and got wax build-up in her poor little ears. She loathed going to the vet because she had to go so often for ear cleanings.

"Are you volunteering for the Adoption Auction this year?" she asked.

"Of course, you know I always do."

"You have a lot going on this year. I'm sorry about Ellie and your business."

"Thanks, we'll be back up and running soon." I hoped.

"Well, maybe you and Ava can offer up a meal for the auction or that delicious pineapple upside down cake that is Opal's secret recipe. I don't suppose I could get you to auction off one of those recipes, could I?"

"You know, a week ago I would have said 'no way,' but today I'd give anything if I could." I grabbed Bobbi Jo and put her in her carrier and shoved the holey duffle bag in my big purse. "Don't worry; we'll come up with something good to auction off."

*

I finished paying for the visit. Ava wasn't in the waiting room. I hoped she hadn't taken off and left me with Bobbi Jo and my bike.

As I walked out of the parking lot, fuming, Keith came toward us with his cocker spaniel, Buddy. Buddy came bounding up to me, pulling Keith along. Bobbi Jo hissed and growled obnoxiously.

"Whoa, Buddy, chillax dude," Keith said, tugging at the leash.

Ava was parked nearby and got out of the car to grab the carrier from me. "I thought you left," I said.

"I didn't feel like being around anyone, and I saw Delilah, and she told me what she told you," Ava said sadly, averting her eyes.

"Hey, Ava," Keith said awkwardly. I could tell he sensed there was something wrong by the nervous shifting he was doing. "Hey, I can leave you two alone; we've got an appointment soon."

Ava began to thank him as I butted in, "No, that's okay. I need to ask you something, Keith." I turned to Ava. "Would you take Bobbi Jo home for me? I'll ride my bike back. Please just take it off the rack and lean it against the building. We can talk later." I turned my back on her, not giving her a chance to reply, and walked in with Keith.

Keith dropped Buddy off with Stacey. He was wearing tight jeans with a purple-and-black flannel shirt and a jean jacket. He turned back to me smiling widely. Tingles ran through my body, giving me goose bumps. I began to shiver.

"Are you cold?" He was already pulling his jacket off when I shook my head.

"No, I'm fine; I just got the shivers momentarily."

"I normally go do something for a bit while they're grooming him. Do you want to get a cup of coffee? I mean tea?" He grinned. I wished he'd stop doing that.

"Sure," I said. "Listen, I saw Denise when I was at the credit union, and she told me something I cannot believe."

"What's that?"

"Did Ellie have stage four cancer and was Lydia the only one who knew? Was she really secretly treating her?"

Keith stopped abruptly on the sidewalk. "How did Denise know that?"

"She told me she overheard the two of you talking."

He shook his head in disgust. "I love living here, but sometimes the small-town gossip drives me nuts!"

"Sorry," I said, looking down at the ground.

"It's not your fault; Denise has always been a nosy Nelly. Yes, it's mostly true. I mean, Lydia is a nurse so she can't treat it on her own, but Ellie wanted Lydia there with her, and she asked that the doctors and techs and nurses keep it private. I'm not sure why Lydia shared it with me. Maybe she felt a lot of the burden not being able to share it with Betsy," Keith said.

Or maybe she was using it as a way to get closer to you.

"You know Ellie never thought I was good enough for you, right?" he asked. "I always took issue with her because of that."

"She was protective of me. She knew the kind of crap I took from my biological father. She wanted me to find someone like my stepdad." My bio-dad, as I unlovingly referred to him, had created a lot of trauma in my early life. My stepdad was a savior; unfortunately, he died of cancer my high school senior year, when I briefly dated Keith. My stepdad died around the time of prom, and I fell apart. I broke it off with Keith and lied to him, telling him I didn't have the same feelings for him as he had for me. I didn't think another senior in high school should have to miss prom and be miserable with me.

"Well, that doesn't make me feel any better that Ellie thought I was like your dad." Keith's face squished up as if he smelled something disgusting. He wasn't joking that he had a dislike for Ellie.

"He was my bio-dad; my dad was Mike," I stated. Ellie had never forgiven Keith for stealing some chocolates from her store on a dare from some of the guys on the football team. She told me anyone like that had no backbone and I was too good for him.

"Ellie had disputes with Lydia too; that may have been another reason she felt comfortable talking to me about it."

"How nice you both have something in common. I'd like to not speak ill of the dead, if you don't mind," I said, tight-lipped.

"Sorry, but Lydia is not so bad. She had a rough childhood," he said in her defense.

I thought about when we were all kids. Lydia spent most of her time at her grandma Clara's place or Betsy's family's house. Her dad had addiction issues from a work accident, and her mom worked all the time.

"We've all got our crosses to bear." I wasn't so eager to defend Lydia.

Stillness filled the air between us.

We walked in silence to a coffee shop on the edge of campus. "It's weird, but you'd probably be dropping by our restaurant since it's right next to the vets."

"Yeah, I didn't want to say anything."

"It's okay. We had the hardest time figuring out what to put on our closed sign. We started with 'closed for murder investigation' and realized that was bad for business, so we settled on 'closed for death in the family.'"

"That's the truth; Ellie and your grandma were like sisters."

"Are you two planning to attend Ellie's funeral?" someone said from behind us and I jumped.

I turned around to see Detective Meiser standing behind us.

"There have been so many things happening in my life, I haven't heard about the details yet," I said.

"I'm Keith; have we met?" Keith reached his hand out to shake the detective's hand.

Meiser grabbed his hand. "Detective Meiser from Tri-City. I'm here helping the chief out for a few weeks on some things."

"Oh right, I remember seeing you in the alley," Keith said.

"Yeah, a lot going on that day." Meiser looked over at me and looked me up and down as my face flushed red.

Keith seemed to notice and put a hand on my back to lead me to a table. "We will get the details, and we will be there; thanks for letting us know," Keith said, purposely moving me away.

I turned and did a half wave. That was awkward.

Chapter Eight

After Keith and I had our drinks, we went our separate ways. I biked back to my house and was taking my helmet off as Ava came walking over in big strides.

"That was rude!" she exclaimed.

"Finding out my best friend may be leaving town from her girlfriend is beyond rude!" I said as tears brimmed in my eyes.

"I know, I'm sorry. I didn't know how to tell you."

"So you are definitely moving?" I asked. "Are you moving to the city?"

"I may be moving to the Dominican Republic—Santo Domingo."

My jaw dropped. I couldn't speak. My body turned into a robot while my head shook back and forth, my ponytail swinging left to right.

"I know, it's a lot to process. Now you know why this was so difficult for me to tell you. I had planned to tell you the other day when everything happened."

"Why?" I managed to squeak out.

"You know my family is from there. They moved here before I was born. My dad has a job opportunity there, and my mom wants to get back there to her family. They want me to go with them to see where our family is from," Ava said, her voice quaking.

"I understand that. I've never been without you. I can't remember a time you weren't in my life," I said, being momentarily narcissistic.

"I feel the same way. That's why the decision is difficult for me. We dreamed up this business and made it a reality. We were off to a great start when all this happened."

"So you haven't decided yet?" I asked.

"No, I have a life here with our business and with Delilah. I'm trying to weigh out my options. But you know I'd never leave you in a lurch. If I decide to go, then we'll work together for you to buy out my half or find another partner."

"If we can't do this together, then I don't want to do it at all."

"Come on, you know that's not true. You are stronger than you think," Ava said, grabbing my hand.

I pulled away from her. All I heard was my bio-dad's voice telling me I wasn't good enough. I felt his absence all the years he was out of my life. At twenty-two, I had hoped I could get his voice out of my head.

"Ava, it's time for you to get home now."

Ava moped out of my room, turning around to thumb her nose at my dad and making me grin.

He shut my bedroom door. "What are you

grinning at?" He picked up the magazines we were looking through and reached for the scrapbook we had been slaving over as we planned out our restaurant for the future.

I grabbed the scrapbook and held it tightly to my chest.

"That's fine, you hold onto your precious book. That's the closest you'll ever get to being successful. You are too dumb to make it happen."

I shook my head out of my reverie. I thought the reality had set in, but when Ava began talking about buying her out and finding another partner my stomach dropped and I felt queasy. "I'm sorry; I can't talk about this right now. It's just too much."

"I know, let's go in, and you can tell me about what you found out. Do you have any more pineapple upside down cake?" Ava asked as we walked in through the kitchen.

"No, my family ate it all," I said, wishing we still had some.

"So, what'd you find out?" Ava asked putting the kettle on.

"Ellie had stage four cancer, and Lydia was one of the only people who knew and was helping with her treatment," I said.

Ava stared at the wall and said nothing for a couple of minutes; I could tell her wheels were turning. "You don't think Lydia did a mercy killing, do you?"

I couldn't believe how often we were on the same page. "I didn't want to believe it. I found it very strange that she wouldn't tell Betsy. I kept thinking if you and I were in this situation there would be no way I couldn't tell you. Yes, my mind has gone there."

"I don't know. We don't know all the details," Ava said.

"I know, but the other thing I thought was strange was that Lydia and Bradley got in that drag-out fight at the crime scene, then I saw the two of them walking into the hospital together being friendly."

"Now, I wouldn't put anything past Bradley," Ava huffed. "What if Lydia and Bradley are in it together?"

"That's a possibility. But just because you and Bradley have had a falling out doesn't mean he's a killer," I said.

"Yeah, and just because you and Lydia are hot for the same guy doesn't mean she's a killer," she said with her eyes slit.

Sometimes we were too much alike for our own good.

"I'm tired, Ava. I saw Detective Meiser today, and he said something about Ellie's funeral. Do you have the details?" I asked.

"Yep, the family decided on no showing, but they are having the funeral tomorrow at Converge Life and Faith Church. It's at 11 A.M."

"Okay, I'll just see you there," I said.

"You don't want to ride together?" she asked.

"Not this time; I need some time alone."

Ava didn't respond, but I caught a tear sliding down her cheek as she turned to leave.

I took the kettle off the stove, deciding I didn't want tea anymore.

I was heading upstairs to have a good cry myself.

Chapter Nine

The next day, Ava came over to my cottage early so we could fix a meal to take to the gathering at the church after Ellie's funeral.

I had made a couple of pineapple upside down cakes last night after I had a good cry. I also made a few deep dish pizzas in the cast iron skillets for the kids who would be there; that way Ava and I wouldn't have to do as much this morning. I had prepped everything for the chili and potato soup we would take today. I was getting ready to put it all in my cast iron Dutch oven pot when the rest of my family showed up.

Normally, they would come in laughing or bickering about something in their noisy way. Today, everyone was dressed in black to mourn Ellie's passing, and they were all quiet. It was already awkward with Ava and me after our not-so-pleasant departure last night. Ordinarily, I loved quietude, but today it was a bit too much.

I grabbed my grandma and hugged her.

"What are you making there?" she asked. My grandma was not one for emotions. The family often joked that we never had to worry about her death because she was so mean. She was a stubborn lady who never had an issue saying exactly what she felt. I've heard people say one loses their filter over time, but Grandma Opal never had a filter.

"I've got a stew and soup I'm throwing together now. I figure if I get it on the stove and in the oven for a bit then the pan will hold the heat until we get to the church and I can put it back on the stove in their kitchen so it will be ready after the funeral."

"Good thinking," my grandma said.

"I learned from the best," I said in an unusual sweet moment with her.

"Mama Opal, why are you the only one who Bobbi Jo is nice too?" Ava asked as Bobbi Jo rubbed against Grandma's leg and purred pleasantly.

Grandma Opal reached down and picked her up, and I noticed Ava's eyes widening. She made a move to stop Grandma, but Bobbi Jo snuggled right into Grandma's bosom and continued to purr. Ava looked shell-shocked.

"She knows I love her, Ava; she doesn't feel any unkindness from me."

"I love her too. I just don't love that she wants to rip my skin to shreds," Ava said.

D.J. Lynn was the next to rub against my mom. My mom cuddled her, scratching under her neck. Ava reached out to pet D.J., and she hissed at her.

"I swear, I have been around this family longer than all you ungrateful cats," Ava bellowed. "You all should be treating me with respect."

That got a laugh out of all the Tucker women.

"Girl, they love you in a completely different way," Aunt Fern said.

"What do you mean?" Ava asked.

"They love to mess with you. You're an easy mark. You get riled up for no good reason, and they think you're funny," Aunt Fern said as the rest of us in the kitchen nodded our heads in agreement.

"Fernie, sometimes you say the dumbest things!" Ava exclaimed.

"You watch your mouth, or I'm not too old to wash it out with soap," Grandma Opal spat out.

Ava did a check of her manners and mumbled an apology to Aunt Fern, who smiled in return.

My mom teared up immediately.

"What's wrong, Mom?"

"Ellie used to say that to Fernie and me when we were little."

The entire kitchen crew went from smiles and laughter back to quietness.

*

The church looked beautiful with white lilies and colorful gladiolus, Ellie's favorite, everywhere. There were pictures of Ellie and her family up in the vestibule with a sign-in book and at the end of each pew inside the nave was a basket of wrapped chocolates from Chocolate Capers. Ellie would have loved that. It wouldn't surprise me if that were Betsy's doing.

"Hey, Jolie." Roxi walked up and grabbed me tightly. Her face was streaked in black from mascara running down her cheeks.

"How are you doing, hon?" I asked as Rex came up behind his sister; his hands were shaking a bit. I never realized how much he cared for Ellie.

"I didn't know her that well, but it was horrible

finding her like that in the dumpster," Roxi said.

"Let's go, sis, I saved us seats in the back," Rex said, guiding his sister.

"I didn't know he was back in town," Delilah said as she and Ava walked up behind me.

"Yeah, he's helping Roxi out with some college course," I said.

"We better get up there, Mama Opal is waving at us," Ava said, grabbing Delilah's hand.

"I'm going to hang back, Ava. You go ahead; I don't feel comfortable sitting with the family," Delilah said.

"Don't be silly, please sit with us," I said, grabbing for her hand.

"No, I'll see you two after." Delilah walked toward her family.

Ava and I moved down the aisle toward my family. "What's that about?" I asked.

"She's trying to distance herself from me in case I leave. She's not out and out saying it, but I know that's what she's doing," Ava said.

"I get it," I said, taking a seat as Ava sat next to me at the end of the pew.

As the minister spoke, I looked around to see many familiar faces. Roxi and Rex nodded to me from the back of the church.

I turned as Grandma began to cry. Her tears made my heart feel like someone was squeezing it too tightly. The woman rarely cried. When my grandpa died, I stayed with her a few nights in the spare bedroom. Grandma woke up from her room and came in to watch me sleep. But I hadn't fallen asleep yet. We had looked at each other momentarily and both broken out into sobs. My mom and Aunt Fern sat on each side of her and wrapped her in their arms. Betsy's mom was up front, nervously looking around the room. She seemed to be scanning all the faces. I found it odd, seeing that this funeral was for her sister. Then I realized I hadn't seen Betsy at all. Betsy would not miss her Aunt Ellie's funeral. She often said she was closer to her aunt than to her mom.

I looked around for Lydia, thinking maybe Betsy was with her. I found Lydia sitting a few rows back, next to Bradley, which again was odd. Roxi sat directly behind Bradley, and she seemed to be staring at him longingly. It looked like someone had a crush.

"Hey, you are being kind of rude," Ava whispered loudly to me.

"Huh? I'm looking for Betsy," I said in an actual whisper.

Ava bobbed her head around and used her full body to turn every which way. And she says I'm the obnoxious one?

"Where could she be? Did she get up and leave from being too emotional?" Ava asked.

"I've never seen her. Honestly, I didn't even notice until I saw her mom looking around the sanctuary nervously," I whispered.

Ava was sitting at the end of the pew and automatically put her hand in the chocolate basket and grabbed a huge handful. She shoved a few over to me. We were both the same in that when we got nervous, we ate. As we unraveled the wrappers, I felt a hard tug on my ponytail from behind.

"Ow," I tried not to be too loud. I turned to see Detective Meiser sitting stoically and eyeballing me like I was an alien from outer space. Next to him sat

Jayjay, who was Dr. Libby's eight-year- old brother. He sat next to Meiser with an annoyed look on his face. He must have pulled my hair.

"Shhhhh." Meiser held a finger to his lips. He pointed to the reverend.

I turned to see the minister pointedly looking at Ava and me while continuing to speak about Ellie's humor. That seemed like an appropriate topic for the moment, considering our behavior.

"You have chocolate all over your face," Ava said.

"What?"

"Chocolate, smeared on your face," she said pointing at my chin.

"Jayjay pulled my ponytail," I said as I turned around to glare at the little boy.

"What a rude kid," Ava stammered, turning to give him the stink-eye.

"Girls, I swear, if you don't put the chocolate down, sit up straight, and mind your manners, I will take you both out of this church and turn you both over my knee." Grandma Opal leaned over, spitting out the words with that bulldog look. Her hands and body were shaking from anger.

I swear I heard Jayjay giggle.

Ava and I instantaneously dropped the chocolate in my bag, sat up, and shut our mouths. Grandma reached over to me to shove a tissue in my hands, and I immediately wiped my face. We behaved for the rest of the service.

*

As I checked on the chili and soup in the kitchen basement that adjoined the church hall, where everyone had gathered to eat and share their best

Ellie moments, I overheard Lydia and Betsy's mom. "The last I saw her was yesterday, when she came to check on me," Betsy's mom was telling Lydia.

"I called her this morning and asked if she wanted me to come over and pick her up for the funeral, but she said not to worry about it, that she had to do something before the occasion," Lydia said.

"She didn't say what?" I asked, completely butting into their conversation.

Lydia glared at me and rolled her eyes, "No, Jolie, she didn't say what she was doing. Don't you think if she told me that I'd be checking on her?"

"Did you try to call her?" I asked.

"We've both been trying to call and text her from the church but the signal is lacking and when I do get through it goes straight to voicemail," Betsy's mom said.

Ava strolled in and said, "Where's Betsy?" at the most inopportune time.

It looked like Lydia wanted to hit Ava upside the head. I'm not sure who would win that fight.

"What's with the look?" Ava huffed.

"We were just talking about that. Jolie, why don't you fill your friend in and I'll go see if I can find her," Lydia said, shaking her head as she strolled off toward the steps.

"What's her problem now?" Ava asked.

"Pretty much anything that has to do with me seems to be a problem with Lydia," I said.

I filled Ava in on the recent conversation.

"You don't think Lydia would do anything to Betsy, do you?" Ava asked.

"What? No, don't be ridiculous!"

"You're the one who thought she killed Ellie to put her out of her misery with cancer!" Ava exclaimed.

"Who are you talking about?" Chief Tobias asked as he walked up with Detective Meiser.

"Um, no one," Ava said sheepishly.

"How did you know Ellie Siler had cancer?" Detective Meiser looked at us both sternly.

"How did you know?" I countered.

"The autopsy," he said matter-of-factly. "So *again*, how did *you* know she had cancer?"

"Jolie told me," Ava blurted out.

I glared at her; so much for protection from friends. "I heard it. I don't believe it was a well-known piece of information. Someone overheard it being mentioned, then told me," I said diplomatically.

"So, the gossip mill," Meiser said.

"*Again*"—I dragged the word out as he did with me a moment ago—"I don't *believe* it was a well-known fact."

"And who is this 'she' you think killed Ellie?" the chief asked.

"Listen, we were just talking. Gossiping, like you said." I nodded toward Meiser. "I'm sure we were overdramatizing the entire thing."

"Well, why don't you let us be the judge of that?" Meiser growled.

"It was Lydia. She knew Ellie had stage four cancer and she was helping to treat her. Jolie thought that maybe Lydia did a mercy killing," Ava blurted out.

I hoped she and I were never kidnapped for information. She'd spill everything.

"You thought I killed Ellie?" Lydia practically shouted.

I had already noticed that many of the folks were beginning to form a line to eat and many were eavesdropping on the conversation.

"I thought you went to look for Betsy," I said, suddenly feeling sick to my stomach. This was getting way out of control.

"I did, Miss Know-It-All, but I saw Rex as I was leaving and he told me he saw Betsy's car at Ellie's house on the way to the funeral. I was going to run over there, but I realized I left my keys down here on the counter," she said, grabbing her keys while simultaneously giving me a look that said she had no issue whatsoever killing me right now.

"You didn't hear the entire conversation. You are making a big deal out of nothing. I am not ratting you out to the police for killing Ellie due to her cancer," I said in a staccato voice.

"What? How can this be?" Betsy's mom cried out.

I swear this day could not get any worse. Why couldn't I keep my big mouth shut?

"Jolie Tucker, what is all the ruckus about? This is the second time today you have embarrassed me. Ellie would have smacked you on your head by now," Grandma Opal said.

"She said Ellie had cancer; did you know, Opal?" Betsy's mom gave my grandma the most helpless look.

"No, she didn't have cancer. She would have told me. She would have told you!" Grandma bellowed.

"She did have cancer. Stage four cancer," Lydia interrupted. "I was helping to treat her, but I did not do a mercy killing."

Suddenly, I was the one who was instigating everything. I was coming completely unglued. Every eye in the room was on me. My breaths begin to get short.

Lydia seemed to be losing it more than me. "Not only that, but I went to visit Grandma Clara in the nursing home, and she told me that those precious Tucker secret recipes never came from your family, to begin with. Opal stole them from Ellie!"

The room was spinning around me. Ava and I stared at my grandma in complete disbelief. My mom and Aunt Fern gasped. Betsy's mom looked like she was ready to faint. I had to get out and get air. I caught my breath in my throat but it was like my body couldn't remember how to let the breath out. I choked as I ran past people, pushing my way to the steps, and then running up two at a time trying to get normal breaths out. I burst through the doors.

Ahhhh, fresh air. I bent over, rubbing my hands along my thighs of my skirt. I stood up tall, working to take deep breaths and to try to make sense of everything that had happened over the course of the last few days. But when my brain tried to work through it all, I felt it was a machine and that a wrench was getting stuck in the gears. I couldn't think right now. I looked across the street. Someone was moving around in Cast Iron Creations.

I slowly walked toward the restaurant, looking around to see if anyone was in the parking lot or if I could see any cars. I went to the side of the building and peeked around to the window. It was Roxi, and she was looking for something.

A voice made me jump. "What's up, Jolie? You look really pale," Rex said.

"You scared me!" I said, my hand over my heart.

"Sorry, I was coming over to pick up Roxi; she said she lost Mom's diamond earring the day the store got closed down. She asked Ava to borrow a key to look for it," he said.

"Teddy doesn't care about the scene?" I asked.

"Sounded to me like you two were back in business," he said.

I looked back toward the church, only to see my grandma being led out the church in handcuffs.

Chapter Ten

I went running across the street. "What is going on?" I demanded.

"Jolie, let us do our jobs, please," Teddy said, gently moving me back.

"Why is she in cuffs?" I yelled. "What happened?"

"I asked your grandmother if the information about the recipes was true," Meiser said.

"No, you made assumptions." Ava had stormed out of the church and was about to pounce on Detective Meiser when Bradley grabbed her around the waist.

"Don't you touch me!" Ava roared.

"Hey, calm down, I'm trying to keep you from getting arrested." Bradley sucked in a breath, trying not to yell.

"So what? Even if the recipes aren't our family's, it doesn't mean she killed her best friend," I said. "You don't live here; you don't know any of us."

"That's right. I'm not biased to your cozy village antics. Now, if you will excuse me, we need to take

our suspect to the station to question her."
Detective Meiser stepped behind Grandma Opal
and grabbed one of her elbows, escorting her to the
back of the police car.

"Grandma, I'm right behind you," I said as I
moved back into the church to retrieve my keys.

"Don't worry about me, Jolie. This will all work
itself out; I didn't do this and the truth will come
out," she said as Meiser pushed her head down as
she got into the back of the car.

"I've got my keys on me, Jolie, let's go," Ava said.

Ava and I followed close behind Meiser to the
station. Ava pulled into a parking space and turned
off the car, sitting still and staring dumbfounded.

I did the same. Neither of us said anything for
what seemed like an eternity.

"Hey, it's going to be okay," Ava said
encouragingly.

"Is it? What has happened to this place? Miss
Siler is murdered behind *our* shop; not only are the
secret recipes missing but now they may have never
even been in my family to begin with. The whole
shop is built around these recipes. And what's
happened to Betsy? I can't believe she wouldn't
show up today. There has got to be something more
going on here; I can't help but think something has
happened to her," I said.

"I know it's crazy right now, but we'll figure it all
out. We've been through everything together, and
we'll get through this too. I agree with you, though,
that something bad has happened to Betsy. Also, I
don't think you should take Lydia's word for
anything; she's been acting weirder than usual
lately," Ava said.

Ava and I jumped as Dr. Libby knocked on my

window. Ava briefly started the car again so she could put the window down.

"What are you two doing here?"

"Weren't you at Ellie's funeral just now?" Ava leaned forward to ask.

"I wasn't able to make it because I had a Great Dane emergency. I wanted to check with the chief to see if it's still okay to move forward with the pet adoption next week. I was planning to head to the church after to pay my respects," Dr. Libby said.

"Oh man, we haven't done anything to help with the campaign. I completely forgot the auction was next week," Ava said.

"That's fine; you two have been dealing with a lot lately. We've got it all moving forward. So much has happened the last few days, I just want to make sure it's okay to move ahead with our plans for the auction before we put more time into it," Dr. Libby said.

"Supposedly, we can open up again, but I never heard it from the chief," I said.

"We are, I was going to tell you at the church. Then all heck broke loose," Ava said.

"What happened?" Dr. Libby asked.

"It's a long story, and I'm not sure I'd be able to rehash the entire thing. Long story short, my family's secret recipes may not have ever been ours, to begin with, and my grandma is now a prime suspect for Ellie's murder," I said as reality set in and tears welled up in my eyes.

"That is ridiculous. Opal wouldn't hurt a soul. I mean, she is petrifying, but it's a humorous kind of scary," Dr. Libby said, hand on hips and her brown ponytail swaying back and forth. "Listen, I'll phone

Teddy later so you can get in there to check on Opal. I'll head over to the church now."

"Bye," Ava and I said in unison as we got out of the little red fiat Ava drove and moved toward the sheriff's office.

*

We were in the waiting area for over an hour, and my leg was bouncing so hard I thought I was going to put a serious indention on the floor.

"What is taking so long?" Ava asked Nancy, the receptionist.

"Ava, for the fifth time, I can't say. The questioning takes as long as it takes and even if I go back there and ask, they aren't going to give me any information," Nancy said.

"This is so stupid; why is this detective from the city in our town anyway?" she asked the ether.

"Well, that I can answer. There's a big controversy where some government officials in Tri-City want to begin urban sprawl," the receptionist said.

"What is urban sprawl?" Ava asked, jerking her head back in confusion.

"They are trying to buy up the rural land between the city and our village to expand the city," Nancy said. "The detective is here on behalf of the Tri-City officials, getting a feel for what farmers and property owners are willing to sell."

"Why send a detective for that kind of work?" I asked.

"Because the mayor of Tri-City is my brother," Detective Meiser said, stepping into the waiting room.

Nancy pretended to busy herself with computer work.

"What exactly is going on here? We've been waiting over an hour. Where is my grandma?"

"I'm sorry, but you will not be able to see her tonight," Meiser said.

"Why not?"

"I'm afraid I can't share with you at this time as to the exact reason why, but your grandma is being charged with the murder of Ellie Siler, and she will need to remain in jail until her arraignment."

The anger in my voice subsided as I said, "When will that be?"

"Should be sometime tomorrow," he said and disappeared into the back of the offices.

*

After calling my mom and speaking to her and Aunt Fern on speakerphone for close to an hour, repeating the same information over and over, I finally lay down on my bed. I was staring at the side of the bed my grandma had slept on the other night.

I wanted to cry, but I think my body was rejecting the tears from too many shed over the last several days, and I drifted off to sleep.

When I awoke, it was pitch black and I was still in my clothes from the funeral. The cats were snuggled up around me. My neck was killing me as I had fallen asleep on my stomach. I sat up to see it was just after midnight. In the bathroom, I splashed some water on my face and put on some comfy sweatpants and a T-shirt. I slipped on my clogs.

I headed downstairs, thinking I would end up in

my kitchen, but I found myself driving toward Cast Iron Creations on autopilot. The clearance we had gotten to open soon was the best news I'd had in the last week.

I parked by the alley and walked back to enter through the rear of the kitchen area. A chill ran down my spine as I looked at the dumpster where Ellie had been found. Normally, Leavensport seemed small and safe. Most of the businesses were within walking distance, and most everyone knew each other. The Friday night football games felt like one big family reunion. But everything appeared different now; it was like a black blanket was dropped on our rural community. Claustrophobia and darkness occupied my body. I hurried into the kitchen and turned on the backlights.

I had never once considered getting an alarm for the restaurant. Now that I was here alone in the middle of the night, I didn't think it was the best decision. I wished we had an alarm I could set.

To take my mind off the fear, I grabbed a tablet and pen and walked around, making a list of what needed to be done before we could reopen. I'd need to go through the food in the refrigerator and see what was good and what needed to be thrown out, and then make a list for the Farmer's Market. I needed to come up with weekly specials for the next couple of months.

I walked to the front of the shop and turned on a lamp near the counter. I looked around to add odds and ends to do to the list. My mind kept wandering to the events of this week. I found my list turning into a list of what had happened.

- *Recipe box goes missing*
- *Ellie is found dead behind our shop in*

our dumpster
- *Lydia and Bradley fight*
- *We have to shut down restaurant*
- *Ellie has cancer*
- *Lydia knew and was helping her with treatment*
- *Lydia and Bradley now get along*
- *Ava is moving FAR AWAY!!!!*
- *Grandma Opal is prime suspect?????*

What more could go wrong? I noticed something oddly shaped sticking out from under a stool at the counter. As I bent down to grab it, a loud crash rang in my ears and I ducked for cover. I was hit on the left side of my body, but I couldn't tell what had slammed into me. Pain coursed through my shoulder down through my hand. Instinct led me to try to move my fingers, but that was a mistake as my entire arm screamed in agony.

I slowly got off the floor to see what had happened, but someone jerked my ponytail back, sending more pain tearing down my left side. My breath caught as the intruder whispered, "Mind your manners and stay out of my business." Before I could do anything, the intruder slammed my head into the wall.

*

What on earth was that ringing sound in my head? I tried to move my head around, but the throbbing and pounding were so uncontrollable that I almost heaved. I slowed my movements as the realization of what had happened came back to me.

How long had I been out? That ringing noise again. What was it? Was my attacker still in here?

That possibility helped motivate me past the pain. I staggered as I tried to stand and held on to chairs and the counter to move back to the kitchen. My plan was to grab a knife in case the intruder was still here. I found out the ringing I was hearing was my cell phone.

"Yeah," I said with a knife in my hand as I looked around.

"I've got her," Ava said. "Where are you? You have me and your family worried sick."

"What time is it?"

"What do you mean what time is it? It's after nine, and we were supposed to meet at your house at eight, so we could decide what all we needed to do before we open again."

"Right, listen, I don't want you to panic, but I need to call the police. There was a break-in at the shop earlier," I said, leaning on the island in the kitchen. It hurt to sit and stand, so leaning seemed like a good compromise right now.

"What, why are you there? Are you okay? Were you there when it happened?" Ava bombarded me with questions.

"I'm okay, but yeah, I was here. I got a little banged up. Let me get off here to call Teddy," I said.

Just then, I heard a knock out front and looked out to see Roxi standing there with a concerned look on her face.

"Nuh-uh you are staying on the line with me," she said as I heard her repeating to my family what I had just said and then I heard my mom in the background phoning the police.

"We are on the way," Ava said. "Stay on the phone until we get there."

"Roxi's out front, Ava. I'm okay. I'm going to let her in," I said, hanging up the phone.

"What on earth happened here?" Roxi said, looking at the broken window, then scanning my body. She quickly grabbed her phone and began punching in a number.

I reached over with my good hand to keep her from calling. "Ava and my family are on their way now; they called the police and I'm sure they called an ambulance too."

"Here." Roxi grabbed a chair and helped me to sit.

I grunted and moved to a sitting position.

"I was going to the art store to pick up some supplies for an art class I'm taking when I saw the window," she said.

All of a sudden, everyone seemed to show up at once. As soon as Ava and my family laid eyes on me, someone called an ambulance. I guess they hadn't called one on the way here.

Teddy asked the standard questions. He found the object that had struck me. It was a large rock with my name written in black permanent marker and a stick figure with a noose around its neck.

That feeling I had in the alley last night came flooding back.

"We need to call someone to come and fix that window in the front door," I said to Ava.

"Yeah, that's top of the list right now," Ava said sarcastically.

"I can do it; please let me help," Roxi said.

"That's sweet of you. Thanks, Roxi," I said.

"We're going to need to take you in, ma'am, and run some scans on that arm," the paramedic said.

*

They ran tests at the hospital and found out I had a cracked scapula, which meant my shoulder blade was fractured. The doctor didn't think I'd need surgery, but he said they'd put a sling on me that I'd have to wear for several weeks. He wanted to see me again in two weeks.

I was lying on the examination table when Lydia walked in with a sling and a script for pain medication.

"Don't worry; I'm not going to kill you."

I rolled my eyes and said nothing. I couldn't deal with this today.

"Dr. Monterey wanted me to show you how to put the sling on and take it off. This is a script for some pain medication. Be sure you don't drive after taking it, and you will want to take it with food."

"Got it. How is Betsy?" I asked, realizing with everything that had happened I never did get to see or speak to her.

"No one knows where she is yet."

"I thought you said Rex saw her car at Ellie's house?"

"It's still there. We've looked at her house, Ellie's house, and everywhere I can think of. I can't find her phone either."

"Aren't you worried?"

"We're all worried sick about her. No one knows if she's missing or if she found another way out of town because of everything that is going on. I know her and I know she would not miss Ellie's funeral. Her mom reported it to Teddy."

"He's not going to have time to look for her seeing that he's arrested my grandmother," I said.

"Hey, I only spoke the truth, and it sounds like they have a right to believe she did it." She paused, looking down with her emerald green eyes and holding up one hand, "No. I am not doing this today."

"What do you mean by that?"

"Jolie, hey, how are you?" Keith walked up to me with a concerned look on his face and began gently rubbing my back. "I just heard what happened and that you were here." He nodded at Lydia.

Lydia did her job in bitter silence, then left the room.

"I'm fine. There is a lot going on right now. I can't talk." I moved to follow Lydia, carefully heading out to demand she tell me what she meant, when I saw her huddled up with Bradley. As I walked toward them, they split apart quickly with Lydia running to the stairs. There was no way I could catch up to her in my condition.

"If I can help you in any way, please let me know," Keith murmured, moving past me awkwardly.

I ignored him, wondering what on earth was going on with Bradley and Lydia.

Chapter Eleven

I went straight to the police station and demanded to speak to Teddy.

"He's not here right now, but let me get the detective for you," Nancy, the receptionist, said.

"Hey, how are you doing? Teddy told me what happened," Meiser said.

That was the nicest he'd been to me since he arrived. "It doesn't matter how I am. What is happening with my grandma? And I don't want to hear that you can't tell me!" My body was shaking all over, and the pain shot through my arm again as beads of sweat formed on my head.

"Sit down and calm down and I'll let you know where we are right now," he said, gently moving me to a small room down the hall. He stopped at a refrigerator and grabbed a bottle of water for me. "Do you have pain pills?"

"I haven't filled the prescription yet. I need to know what is going on," I said, desperately feeling the room spin from the pain and panic of the events.

"The reason things took so long last night is we got a warrant to search your grandma's house. We didn't even have to go inside. We found the recipe box hidden inside a bench on her porch."

My mind spun. "She didn't do it."

"No one is saying she did it at this point, but the evidence points directly at her, and we need to hold her while we continue to investigate," he said softly.

"I want to see her. Right now. I want to see her," I moaned.

"Teddy has her in a holding cell in the back, and no one is with her or around her right now. He wants to keep her there as long as he can while we finish investigating. You can go back and speak to her, but you only have fifteen minutes."

I got up to move, and the room began spinning again. Out of habit, I tried to use my left arm to help steady myself and howled in agony. Here came the tears again.

Meiser reached out quickly and grabbed my waist. "Why don't you let me take you to get your prescription filled so you can take your pain meds, then I can bring you back here to talk to your grandma when you are doing better?"

"No, I'm fine. I just need to slow down. Take me back there."

He kept an arm around my waist, and I couldn't help but lean on him, even though it was the last thing I wanted to do. He led me to grandma's cell and grabbed a chair for me.

Grandma Opal jumped and reached through the bars. "What happened to you?" she yelped.

"It's a long story, Grandma. I promise I'm fine, and I'll tell you everything when we get you out of here. But right now, I only have fifteen minutes with you. So, please, let me find out how you are doing."

"Oh, I'm okay. They feed me, and there aren't any crazies in the cell with me. The bed is horrible and hurts my back. I have Teddy figuring out if he can get my meds for me to take while I'm in here. Don't worry about me, I didn't do this. I'll get out of this mess yet," she said with that stubbornness that usually drove me batty but today made me feel proud to be her granddaughter.

"I know you didn't do this, but Grandma, you need to tell me about the recipes. Is what Lydia said true? No beating around the bush. I need to know if those recipes are our family's or not," I said, glancing up at the clock.

Grandma looked me straight in the eye through the bars. "Nothing is ever as it seems and most situations are more complicated than what people think."

"I said no beating around the bush; now tell me what is going on right now!" I demanded in anger.

To my surprise, my grandma grinned at my fury, which only made me more livid.

"You are too cute when you're upset. You get that same look in your eyes that your grandpa used to get. Don't get me wrong; most anybody would be frightened—it's a crazy look—but not me. I know your heart," she said, reaching out to stroke my hair.

"I know; I need to get a perm." I couldn't help but grin.

"Yes, do that first. Second, I've visited with your mom and Fernie, and I talked them into going ahead with the upcoming Adoptions for Strays. The

Tucker family has never missed one year since Dr. Libby started this and we aren't going to start now. We are pet-friendly and always will be. So they know the plan, and I expect you to follow it!" she exclaimed.

"I can't think about that right now; there are too many other things going on," I said, defeated.

"Jolie, your time is up. I'd like to run you to the pharmacy for your pain pills and take you home," Detective Meiser said.

Grandma eyeballed him up and down and smiled. "Well, Jolie, you can't refuse an offer like that. Now, you get on out of here and go get drugged up with this nice young man."

My eyes about bulged out of my head. Did my grandma really tell me to go get "drugged" up with the guy who was trying to put her away?

Meiser, with an amused look, helped me up. I went to the bars and reached through to hold her hand, then kissed it, telling her I loved her and I would figure this out.

As I leaned on Meiser and we walked out, my grandma's voice rang out down the hall, "Be sure to use protection."

"I like her," he said, laughing under his breath.

Grinning and looking up at him, I said, "She's a handful; believe me, you will be begging me to take her back soon enough."

"I have no doubt!"

*

After I got home and took the pain medicine, I was out of commission for a couple of days. Everything that had happened the last week had caught up with me. The beating I took the other night did me in, and my entire body ached as if a virus of some sort was coming on. Plus, I never did well on painkillers. They made me feel sick to my stomach, but I had to keep taking them. I spent two days in bed in a fog of depression and pain meds.

The off-and-on depression had been the story of my life as far back as I could remember. My bio-dad really did a great job of messing me up. I've always been different from the norm. My doctor wanted me to take medication for social anxiety as a kid. I struggled when having to be in front of people to speak, and I was most comfortable alone. Being around Ava and my family was fine, but even that created more stress for me than it seemed to for others.

Sometimes it was every few weeks and sometimes every few months. I would go into a funk and have to hole myself up at home and be alone. It freaked my family and Ava out, but they had learned over time the best thing they could do for me is let me be and let it run its course. I struggled to trust most people, especially men. Socializing took a lot of energy out of me and the last week had definitely taken me out of my comfort zone.

Although the physical pain was still there, I had recouped from the depression and found the strength to move on. I finally took a shower and put fresh clothes on, grabbing my worn jeans, ankle lace-up gray leather boots, and my favorite Pan America sweatshirt, which had an image of cast iron skillets making up all fifty states of America. I used the curling iron to curl my hair and pulled it up for volume. My grandma was right. When all this mess was figured out I needed a perm!

I drove carefully to Cast Iron Creations, where I

knew Ava and my family were working to get ready for our reopening. I hadn't had a chance to talk more with Ava to see if she'd decided to move.

It always amazed me how quickly the leaves fell and the trees went bare during the fall. Everything had been turning beautiful colors last week, and this week most of the leaves were falling, leaving some of the trees bare. Every year, I wanted the colorful leaves to last longer. I needed to learn to appreciate when things were good.

At the restaurant, the glass had been fixed. Roxie and Ava must have taken care of all that.

"What's going on, ladies?" I asked as I walked in on what seemed to be a secret huddle.

"You don't look too bad today. Your makeup looks nice; it looks like you curled your hair some," my mom said, grabbing her camera and getting up close to get my picture.

"Thanks?" I questioned the half compliment as I squinted from the flash. "Why are you taking my picture?"

"Can't a mom want some pictures of her kid?"

"What is happening right now?" I asked Ava with my right hand on my hip.

"Girl, I got some new lipstick that you have got to try; let me grab it out of my purse ...Where did I put it? Ah, there it is! Cherry Ripple and it's a deep sexy red," Ava said, walking up to me with lipstick aimed at my lips.

"I'm okay, but thanks," I said, putting my right hand up to fend her off.

"I want to see what it looks like on you; let me try some," Aunt Fern said slathering the lipstick all over her lips. It was going a little off her lips in places, making her look like a mad clown. She wasn't helping Ava's case at all.

"Okay already, I give in; please just let me put it on myself," I said, swatting at Aunt Fern as she reached for my lips with the Cherry Ripple.

I said with that voice women make while talking and putting lipstick on, "I see you got the window fixed, thanks."

"No worries, I knew you needed some time to recover. Roxi made the call and I was here when they came," Ava said. "Let us see."

I turned to have my mom's phone back in my face as she clicked pictures, "Mom, stop." I sounded like a child whining.

"Beautiful," my mom said.

I stood for a moment and looked at the three women, who wore looks of anticipation. "What's the plan?"

"The plan?" Ava asked innocently.

"Yeah, *the plan* that Grandma Opal told me I had to follow."

"Child, you are so dramatic! You act like we are the police investigating you or something," Aunt Fern said.

"Okay, family, so let's have it. What do you need to ask me?"

"Well, we were wondering if you would help us out with our family's booth for auctioning night," Mom asked.

"Of course. That's it? Ava and I would be happy to do a gift certificate, or we could make a romantic dinner for two," I said, throwing out a couple of options.

"That's great, really great, that you will help out,"

Aunt Fern said.

"I don't understand why you all are making such a big deal out of this," I said, shaking my head.

"Because we don't want your food, Jolie. We want to auction you off for a date at the Tucker booth," Aunt Fern blurted out.

"What? No, not going to happen." I tried to cross my arms, but I was still sore, so I shook my head back and forth in defiance.

"Now, Jolie, you know it's been forever and a dime since you've had yourself a nice man in your life. It's time, girl. This auction is a great opportunity . . ." my mom said, interrupting my tantrum.

"To what? Auction off your daughter to the highest bidder?" I raised my eyebrows.

"We aren't saying that you have to marry the guy that bids the highest, but geez Louise, at least go out on a date. Maybe Keith will make a bid," Aunt Fern said, wagging her bushy eyebrows.

"All of a sudden everyone has an opinion on Keith and me," I said.

"Who is everyone? You're overdramatic again!" Mom exclaimed.

"Oh, I don't know, Denise mentioned something about it at the credit union earlier last week."

"Well, then it sounds like fate to me," Aunt Fern said. Ava was unusually quiet. "So, you're in on this too?" I asked.

"Well, I think it sounds good. You need to get out, girl. Was this Mama Opal's idea?" Ava suddenly perked up.

"Yes, and she was adamant about all of us making this happen," Mom said, staring me down with that withering mother stare. "Don't tell me you are going to go against your own grandmother's wishes while she rots away in jail."

"Geesh, Mom, don't resort to a guilt trip or anything," I said, rolling my eyes. "Fine, I give in; I'll do it. I am going to run to the farmers market and pick up a few things. Suddenly, I feel like I need to get some air."

"So, you're feeling better now?" Ava asked.

"I'm moving on. I guess I should let you all know that if Ava decides to leave, then I've decided to close the restaurant."

"Jolie, come on . . ." Ava pleaded.

"No, I'm not punishing you. We can open back up temporarily while we figure it all out, Ava. You do what is right for you. I will be fine. I'll figure out my next move," I said, giving my bravest smile. "Now, I really do want to get to the farmers market."

"Sounds good, dear. We'll talk about this decision later. Don't forget the auction is tomorrow night, so make sure you wear something nice," Mom said as I slowly rolled my entire head around. An eye roll seemed way too tame for this moment.

*

After picking up some provisions for the next day, I decided to go the long way and drove east by the edge of town to drive by Meadow Falls Park. Many of the trees were beginning to go bare, but the ground of the park was littered with bright colors from the leaves that had recently fallen. There was a sign up on land by the park and it said "SOLD" on it. I hadn't even known it was up for sale. I pulled over and looked closer at the sign—five acres had been sold, mostly flat land with lush, green grass and a sprinkle of trees throughout the property. I wondered if this had to do with the planned urban sprawl. I completely understood that concept, but thought it would start near the city and move into town, not the other way around. I looked at all the farmland and the woods out toward the horizon. I hadn't been back in those dense woods since we were kids and used to go to the cabin. Whoever bought this land had picked a prime spot for beautiful scenery with the brownish-yellow farm fields leading into the thick wooded area where large shadows loomed from the towering trees—as long as it was going to stay that way.

Chapter Twelve

Ava and I were doing a little more work to the restaurant to get it ready to temporarily reopen on Monday morning. Even though I had dark clouds hanging over me, the thought of getting back to work helped to lighten my load. I couldn't help but wonder what the real story was with the recipes and if the answers would shut us down while embarrassing the family. Not to mention, I might no longer have a co-owner …Uh, and Grandma; when would I see her again in a normal setting?

"Hello, Jolie, are you in there?" Ava asked, waving a hand in front of my face.

"Sorry, my mind was wandering," I said, vowing to myself to put these disturbing thoughts out of my head for the moment.

"Yeah, I'd say! I was asking what you were going to wear tonight for the auction."

"Oh, I haven't even given it a single thought with everything else going on," I said, thinking I had better begin figuring it out as it would be time to get ready in just a few short hours. "I'm going to go to the back and double-check everything is in order and make sure I have everything on the list to get at the store tomorrow."

I wanted to look through the hand-carved recipe box my great-grandmother had passed down. The box was a beautiful wooden vintage masterpiece. It had a Bohemian floral print carved on all sides of the box. The recipe cards were antiquated as well, with pretty pink flowers at the bottom of each card, and the coloring had dulled over the decades of use. Great-grandma had typed in each recipe all those years ago. Since then, Ava and I had created our own recipes and I played with a few of the recipes to modernize them. I had thought about dividing the recipes up by the most modern that Ava and I had created up front and the oldest recipes all together in the back of the box. I hated that the police were holding it as evidence. I was adding the few grocery items to my list when Ava yelled back, "We need to head home to get ready for the auction. We'll have to finish up in the morning."

"Okay, I'm coming," I said as I walked through the swinging doors to the front. I took a moment to look around and my eyes landed on the painted mural on the side wall of the village that Delilah had painted a year ago when we opened. It brought tears to my eyes remembering how proud Ava and I had been and thinking now of what our future could hold. All of this could be over within a few short months.

"Did you decide what you are wearing tonight? You know you really need to dress up nice to make money for the strays for the pet adoption that will be coming up. So don't wimp out and wear a turtleneck or anything," Ava said.

"Got it," I said, thinking I couldn't wait to get this night over.

*

After I went home and changed, I ran by Betsy's apartment to see if she happened to be there. Betsy's mom still didn't know what to think about her daughter's disappearance. The last I had heard, she had filed a missing person report with police.

When I saw she wasn't home, I went to Lydia's apartment, which was in the same complex, to see if she had any word on Betsy. I knocked on the door and Bradley answered.

"Uh, hi, Jolie," Bradley stammered, "Lydia, Jolie is here," he yelled to the back of the apartment where the bedroom was located. He swept a hand to the inner room, signaling me to come in.

The apartment was warm and cozy, with big cushioned furniture in warm fall rusts and greens. It seemed to contrast Lydia's personality.

"What is she doing here? You didn't answer, did you?" Lydia said, stomping down the hall to the living room area.

"Yeah, he answered," I said.

"Oh, what do you need?"

Poor Bradley looked like he was caught between a rock and a hard place.

"I stopped by Betsy's place hoping she would be there, but she wasn't. I thought I'd drop by to see if you heard from her yet."

"No," Lydia said and averted her eyes to Bradley momentarily as he stood there awkwardly.

"Don't elaborate or anything," I said. "What exactly is going on between the two of you? First, you both are having a drag-out fight in the alley. Next, I see you huddled up walking into the hospital together; you're both at Ellie's funeral sitting together, and now Bradley's at your apartment. There is something you aren't telling me."

Bradley began to speak, but Lydia shut him down with her hand held up to his face. "It's really none of your business. I know we all used to be close, but that was when we were kids. We aren't kids anymore eating s'mores by the fire and giggling. We're all grown up now with jobs and lives. You and I haven't been close in a long time, and I resent you thinking you can butt into my business."

"Why don't you tell me how you really feel," I said. "Okay, all I want to do is figure out what is going on with Betsy. If you two want to keep being the Hallmark mystery movie of the week, then that is fine with me. I'll figure out what's happening on my own."

"No one asked for your help," Lydia spat out.

"Not everything is about you, Lydia. My grandma is in jail right now for Ellie's murder; Betsy is missing; my best friend may be moving far from me." I paused, trying to keep my cool. "I'm just trying to figure out what is happening. I'm trying to save my grandma, my family's heritage, and my business. Why don't you give me a break!"

"Listen, Jolie, I know you have a lot going on right now. I felt bad about the way I acted in the alley, and I apologized to Lydia. Beyond that, I'm working on a breaking story right now, and she has some information. That's all I can tell you," Bradley said, trying to ease some of the tension out of the air.

Lydia scowled at him.

"Does your story have to do with Ellie's murder

or helping my grandma?" I asked.

"He's not going to answer that!" Lydia exclaimed, glaring at Bradley and then moving her cold eyes to me.

We had a momentary standoff. "That's fine," I said, calmly taking a breath. "I need to head to the auction anyway."

"I won't be too far behind," Bradley said, again trying to shrug off the animosity.

"You're not going?" I was tempting fate by asking Lydia yet another question.

"I have other things to do," she said.

*

I was uncomfortable walking into the auction in my jade green dress and black pumps. The dress was shorter than what I normally would wear, not that I wore dresses that often. Ava had talked me into buying it a couple of years ago for a wedding, but I never ended up wearing it. I was pleasantly surprised that it still fit, even if it was a bit snug on my hips, which made it rise a little more. But the lacy black floral chiffon was loose and hung a bit below the hem of the dress. Tonight, I went all out like Ava had demanded earlier, styling my long and now-flat dark blonde locks up in a loose bun and allowing some curls, which I got with my trusty curling iron, to fall around my face. Normally I didn't wear much makeup, but tonight I went all out with eyeshadow, mascara, *and* lipstick, the Cherry Ripple.

Ava ran up to me as I walked in. "Girl, you look fab-u-lous! Wow, what a knockout! I never knew you could look so good."

"Thanks ...I think."

"Dr. Libby will have a lot of money to take care of adopting out those strays with that dress you're wearing," Ava said and chuckled.

"You are the one who talked me into buying this dress. This is the first time I've worn it."

"Well, I have good taste," Ava said. "Come on; I'll show you where your family's booth is."

As Ava dragged me to the booth, I heard catcalls and whistles from my family. The heat rose to my face. "Oh be quiet, you guys; I will never forgive any of you for this," I said, grinning at them. I was saddened not to see my grandma there.

My mom pulled me aside momentarily. "Have you heard anything from Betsy or where she is yet?"

"I haven't," I said, moving back to the Tucker clan. "Anyone heard anything about Betsy lately?"

Aunt Fern and Ava both shook their heads in unison with concerned looks.

I thought of Lydia's recent comment about s'mores at the cabin when we were kids and asked my mom and Aunt Fern, "Do you two remember when Grandma and Ellie used to take us girls to Ellie's cabin when we were kids?"

"Of course I remember that! You kids had the best time at the campfires and singing songs, and we used to make up stories. Boy, those were the days!" Mom exclaimed.

"Is the cabin still back in the woods?" I asked.

"As far as I know it is. I don't believe Ellie ever sold it, and I would imagine it would be listed in her will," Aunt Fern said.

"Jolie, turn around," my mom said.

I turned around and my mom snapped more photos. "Mom, why are doing this again?"

"I'm taking your picture. You look beautiful."

I mumbled under my breath. "You don't take my picture any other day; only when you're trying to sell me off to the highest bidder."

"Hey, do you have a minute for me now?" I felt a tug on my good elbow and turned around to see Keith dressed in a black tuxedo.

"Wow, you look terrific," I said as we moved away from my family.

"Me, what about you?"

"Thanks, Ava talked me into buying this dress for a wedding before and I thought I'd give it a try for tonight's auction."

"You look good in the dress, but you look great in anything," he said, blushing.

"I'm sorry I was so short with you at the hospital. That was really nice of you to come and check on me. Heck, it seems like all you've been doing lately is checking on me for one thing or another."

"It's okay. I know you've had a lot on your plate lately. I just wanted you to know that I'm here for you if you need anything," he said, smiling at me.

I felt goose bumps going up and down my arms again. It created a bit of a painful sensation in my left arm and I winced.

Keith made a gentle move toward me, but I pulled away.

"I'm okay, really," I said.

He gave a half-hearted smile and walked away with his hands in his pockets.

*

I pulled Ava out of the main room into the hallway by the kitchen. I swore I saw the closet door creak shut. I was still paranoid from the attack at the restaurant. I kept thinking someone was watching me. I shook off the moment of fear. "Hey, I'm going to make a quick run to Ellie's cabin to see if Betsy may be there."

"That's a good idea. It would be great if she had just taken off to get some space. I can go with you tomorrow," Ava said.

"No, now," I said holding up a hand in protest when I saw the annoyed look on her face. "I know you are worried about me being back in time for the auction. Don't worry; I plan to run by it and see if anyone is there. Plus, tomorrow will be too crazy with doing all the last-minute things before opening back up our restaurant. I have to run to the store in the morning, then prep before we open. I won't be able to enjoy myself tonight until I check," I said firmly.

"You better be back for your time slot for the auction," Ava said.

"I will. The auction hasn't even started, and I'm listed toward the end," I promised. "I know I'm probably just being silly, but I won't be able to relax until I check. See you soon." I gave Ava a quick hug and headed out to my car.

Chapter Thirteen

I drove past the land that had sold by the park and noticed a large black truck sitting off to the side of the road. I wondered if another villager was doing what I had done the other day, questioning the land being sold. As I drove back toward the woods, I began to plan for the restaurant's temporary reopening. I needed to try and talk to whoever the new owner was of Chocolate Capers, Jenni from Jenni's Diner, and some of the other proprietors of eateries in the village about how we could all work together to cross-sell each other's products. The one thing I hated about owning a restaurant in a small village was the feel of competition. If all of the owners worked together, we could keep that small village homey. This would be one of the last positive things I could contribute to the village before shutting down or selling for good.

I came out of my musing and realized I had turned down the wrong road in the woods. I turned around to try the next road. It had been years since I had been back here, which was weird because it wasn't really that far from the village and it was beautiful. There were many graveled paths for hiking or mountain biking and the roads were still in great shape. A few minutes later I slowed down as I saw the cabin and the long narrow road to get to it. I drove up the rickety lane and noticed smoke coming out of the chimney. I pulled my car off the side of the lane and turned my lights off.

I quietly moved out of my car, lightly closing the car door with my one good arm, and moved toward the cabin. I was afraid I might break my ankles in my heels on the dark, gravelly drive and I did stumble once or twice, but eventually I reached the side of the cabin. I headed toward the side window, thinking back to when the other three girls and I would play hide-and-seek in the woods. A smile crept up as I thought of better times.

I peeked inside the window and my eyes widened as I saw Betsy tied up to a chair. She was looking straight at me, mouthing something to me that I couldn't make out. Betsy shuffled in the chair; her body writhed around in panic. As I turned to head to the front of the cabin, I was grabbed from behind and a hand went to my mouth. I turned to see Lydia glaring at me.

I kept feeling my phone buzz from inside my sling where I had put it, and I went to grab the pepper spray that I kept on my keyring when she backed up and said, "What are you going to try to do, blind me?"

My phone buzzed again. "Why do you have Betsy? You did kill Ellie, didn't you?" I cried out.

"Be quiet, and turn that phone off and put that pepper spray away now! Have you lost your mind completely?" she seethed. "I'm here to *save* Betsy."

I still didn't completely believe her as I glanced from Betsy inside to Lydia.

"Look," Lydia said as she grabbed my head to keep me ducked below the windowsill.

I peeked in and saw Roxi standing by the fire. My mind went completely blank. There went my phone again, this time ringing.

"Turn it off," Lydia screeched. "You're going to get us caught!"

"Too late for that."

We both whipped around from the window to see Rex holding a gun on both of us.

*

Rex kicked open the cabin door and shoved both Lydia and me forcefully through it, sending us flying to the hardwood floors, where I scraped my knees and felt another jolt of pain fly down my arm.

"Oh no, I just feel *horrible* about your pretty little green dress, you nosy little witch," Rex seethed.

I looked down and saw my dress had a tear in it. I looked toward Betsy, whose mascara had streaked down her face. Roxi stood in silence, panic and fear pasted all over her face. "Rex, what is going on here?" I asked as calmly as possible, trying to buy time and distract him from that gun in his hand. A part of me hoped Ava might come looking for me, but at the same time I feared that my best friend would be in jeopardy if she came out here.

"Do you think I wanted any of this to happen?" Rex paced back and forth and waved the gun around with wild eyes.

As Rex began talking, I looked around the room for any weapons or opportunities to get Betsy, Lydia, and me out. I had shoved my keys in my sling with my phone when we were out in the dark, but Rex had heard my phone and taken it from me. I still had the pepper spray, though. Lydia and I made eye contact, and she looked over next to her at the poker by the fire, but Roxi was standing right there.

"I didn't want to kill anyone," Rex continued. "I had it all: quarterback, girls, a cushy life." He suddenly stopped and whipped around, looking toward the window and then back to his sister. "Did you hear that?" He was talking a mile a minute.

"No, Rex, come on, calm down and think. You are turning paranoid," Roxi said. "You are spiraling out of control. You didn't mean to kill Ellie; it was an accident. I told you we should have called the police."

Rex's face was turning bright red and sweat poured off of him.

"You don't look so good," I said and glanced over at Roxi in concern.

"Shut up!" he screamed and took two long strides toward me. He pulled at my bun and put his body, which ranked of sweat, against mine. "Or I'll break that other arm of yours."

"He's high," Lydia interrupted.

Rex stepped back wild-eyed and rubbed his free hand through his hair in agitation.

Roxi looked down at Lydia. "How do you know that?"

"I'm a nurse, and he came into the hospital last week to be treated for heart palpitations. His behavior mimics those of a cocaine addict," she said, looking Rex in the eye. "You should know that Bradley knows about your suspension from the football team and that you are on academic probation; he's planning to write a story on it."

Rex moved like a cat and pounced on Lydia, putting the gun against her forehead. "How does your boyfriend know all this?"

"He's friends with the coach; plus, it doesn't take a genius. You are starting quarterback; there has been a game, and you weren't in it," she said in a tone I don't believe I would use with someone who had a gun at my head.

"Why did you kill my aunt?" Betsy asked.

That seemed to take his attention away from Lydia. "Like Roxi said, it was all an accident. I was suspended and back home. I was supposed to pick Roxi up from work. I went to the back alley to—"

"Get high," Lydia finished for him.

"Yeah." He gave Lydia a nasty look. "She had some sort of dog and cat things in her hands and said she was looking for Opal. I thought she didn't notice. If only she hadn't seen me. I told my parents that I couldn't keep my grades up. I didn't want anyone to know. She had to say something about it," he said, pacing furiously again and rubbing his hand through his hair.

"She cared about you. She was concerned," Betsy spit out angrily.

"Well, it was none of her business! Just like it was none of your business," he said, pointing the gun at Betsy carelessly.

"So, you lied to me at the funeral, in the parking lot," Lydia said.

"Yeah, I had Roxi move the car to Ellie's driveway, and I brought her here," he said, pointing to Betsy.

"How'd you know about the cabin?" I asked.

"She told me about it," he said, pointing to Roxi.

"I had heard you and Ava talk about it a while ago and when he told me he had Betsy, he wanted to kill her. I didn't know what to do. I talked him into letting me bring her here while we figured it all out," Roxi said through tears. "I'm so sorry, Jolie. When I found out what he did to you, I came straight to the restaurant to make sure you were okay. I was trying to save Betsy too."

"I told her how to get here. I was thankful that she helped to spare my life," Betsy said, looking at Roxi and giving her a slight smile.

That was smart. We needed to get Roxi on our side, and then we'd have a better chance at persuading Rex to let us go.

"Roxi, I know this has all gotten out of hand. I think if we all put our heads together, we can figure out how to salvage this mess," I said, looking from Roxi to Rex. "You said it yourself—it was an accident, right?"

"She's not going to help you. Roxi is the one who told me you were on your way; she heard you talking to your annoying sidekick at the auction," Rex spat as a deep redness moved from his neck to his face.

"Rex, let me talk!" Roxi said.

He cut her off. "Yes, Ellie offered to take me to the hospital to get in a drug rehab program; I was high and paranoid. I ran at her, and she tried to grab me. When I shoved her, she fell and hit her head on the corner of the dumpster. I couldn't believe how fast it all happened. There was so much blood. I never knew someone could bleed that much," Rex said, staring off in space like he was reliving the moment.

"She was on anticoagulants because she was at

risk for blood clots with her cancer; that's why she bled out so quickly," Lydia said.

"I'd never seen anything like it," Roxi said.

"You were there?" I asked, stunned.

"I wasn't there when it all happened. I was closing up that night because Ava needed to meet Delilah. She gave me her key. I thought he would be waiting for me up front. I couldn't find him, so I went to the back and saw him standing there over the body," Roxi wailed. "She had her dog and cat molds. One of them fell out of the dumpster when Rex threw her in, and I grabbed it. I thought it could be something to remember her by," she said, looking off in contemplation.

"That's what I saw the other night at the restaurant. There was an odd-shaped silver thing lying under the stools; I went to pick up, and that's when the rock came flying through the window," I said.

"I had it with me when I went to take the recipe box back the day of Ellie's funeral, and I must have dropped it," Roxi said.

Again, my mouth dropped open slack-jawed. "You stole the recipe box?" I said.

Roxi looked at the ground as her cheeks flushed red. "It was stupid. I was trying to make it right."

"But ...why?" I stammered.

"I have a crush on Bradley. I overheard him talking to one of his friends at the campus coffeehouse one day. He was talking about Ava and Delilah, and how he'd like to pay back Ava for the pain and embarrassment she put him through. Like I said, it was stupid."

"So, you decided to steal the recipe box from the

restaurant?" I asked.

"I saw you pulling it out of a tile one morning when I got there early. I figured I'd tell him I knew all about him and Ava and so I took the recipe box. I was going to let him decide how he wanted to use it. I thought that might help him to notice me," she said. "But the day of Ellie's funeral, I went back to the restaurant to put it back. Everything had gotten out of control."

"That's the day I saw you were snooping around," Rex said to me.

"It's my restaurant," I said.

"After everything happened, we made a copy of Ava's key in case we needed to get back inside," Roxi said.

"I told you she borrowed Ava's key and I figured you'd figure out I was lying. I had to shut you up," Rex said, which explained the rock through the window with my name and the drawing of the noose and the attack.

"When I saw your grandma being arrested, it was perfect. I took the box from Roxi and drove to her house and put it on her porch," Rex said with a smile.

That smile really ticked me off. "So, let me get this straight. Because you are a narcissistic little punk with no self-control, you killed an old lady who had stage four cancer, framed another old lady of a murder, kidnapped a grieving niece, attacked me, and now you are holding us all at gunpoint? Does that about sum it up, genius?" I asked.

Bradley flew toward me and grabbed my hair, putting the gun right at my temple. "You think you are so smart with your stupid, happy little family. Not everyone who grows up in Leavensport village lives in your little rainbow and unicorn world," he said, rage filling his eyes.

I reached for my pepper spray at the same moment Lydia reached for the poker. She hit Roxi in the head with it and turned to hit Rex next but he ducked, still holding onto my hair. I pointed and sprayed, but it missed him and went into the fire, causing a small flare-up. That distracted him, and Lydia again swung the poker, this time hitting him squarely in the back of his head. Rex fell to the floor as the gun flew from his hand. He wasn't knocked out completely, and we fought for the gun. I didn't even notice the pain in my arm from the adrenaline, and I took my foot with the heel and jammed it where the sun doesn't shine. Rex screamed out in pain as Lydia stood over him and hit him again, knocking him out this time.

Chapter Fourteen

The next week ran much smoother. It was Monday, two days after the fiasco at the cabin, and Cast Iron Creations was back in business and running strong. We had closed down at the end of the workday and Betsy, Lydia, Bradley, Keith, Ava, and I were all enjoying some of the leftover pineapple upside down cake I had made, with some beverages to celebrate the first day of the reopening.

"I was freaking out when I couldn't reach you on the phone the other night," Ava said.

"Nice job, Ava. You calling your friend got us caught," Lydia said gruffly as she shoved a forkful of cake into her mouth.

"I was worried. I didn't know a coked-out maniac was at the cabin," Ava grunted.

"I was happy I thought to take my phone with me. I called the police after Lydia knocked him out. I am sad to see Roxi is being charged as an accessory, though," I said. "I couldn't believe that pepper spray created a small eruption when it hit the fire."

"You must have bought one where some of the

active ingredients have alcohol in them. That would cause that," Bradley said.

"How on earth do you know that?" Lydia asked, seeming impressed.

"I did a story on women and self-defense, and I did some research on the best pepper sprays to buy. By the way, it's best not to buy the ones with alcohol," he said.

"In this case, it seemed to work for us," I said, grinning at Lydia.

"So, Roxi had a crush on me?" Bradley asked, seeming a little flattered.

"So much so that she was willing to steal our secret recipes," I said.

"The recipes are yours then?" Keith asked.

"Mostly," I said, taking a deep breath to repeat what my grandma had explained to me yesterday when she visited my house. "Grandma said that when she and Ellie were around our age, they wanted to use the recipes to start a business similar to what Ava and I have done. Many of the recipes did come from my family, but Ellie and Grandma altered some of them and created some of their own cast iron recipes together."

"So, why didn't they end up opening a business?" Betsy asked.

"Well, Grandma said it was a different time then. She was married and had kids and felt her place was at home while my grandpa worked for the railroad. Ellie never married, so she ended up starting the chocolate shop. Grandma said Ellie didn't have the heart to do the cast iron restaurant without her." I smiled as a rush of emotion ran through me thinking about Ellie. "Ellie told Grandma to keep all the recipes they created together and to pass them down to her kids and grandkids. She had hoped maybe someday someone in our family would do what they were never able to do." I was beginning to get choked up.

"And here we are, large and in charge," Ava belted out, holding her arms out.

Bradley rolled his eyes. "Please tell me you decided to move," he said playfully.

It seemed those two might be getting past the ugliness of their relationship. I hoped that Bradley and Delilah could work out their differences too.

"You wish! After everything that happened the last two weeks, it helped me get my priorities straight. This is my home. I'm going to miss my family a lot, but my dad will be making good money, so he said he'd pay for my airfare for visits a few times a year. Mom, Antonia, and I will Facetime, talk, and text all the time, I'm sure," she said.

"I'm so happy you aren't going anywhere," I said, trying to reach to put my arm around her. But my body was still banged up and bruised from the further abuse Rex had done to me at the cabin, so I just patted her shoulder. I was also thrilled to know the business was open for good.

"Speaking of big life decisions," Betsy said, "Aunt Ellie would be thrilled to know I am taking over Chocolate Capers."

"You are! Oh, that's so exciting," I squealed.

"Yeah, I'm going to continue to be a nurse for now, but I'm going to be a silent partner," Lydia said.

"Are you sure you know how to be silent?" I asked.

She frowned at me.

I dropped my napkin, on purpose, to avoid her gaze and when I went to pick it up, I noticed that Bradley and Lydia were holding hands under the table. Hmmm ...It looked like there might be a budding romance!

"Betsy, I was thinking the other day that all the entrepreneurs in our village who sell food items should get together so we can find ways to cross-sell our products. Would you be willing to help me get everyone together and come up with ideas?" I asked.

I was taken aback to see Betsy's eyes fill with tears. "That is one of the last conversations I had with Aunt Ellie. She had mentioned using her chocolates to make some pies, cakes, and cookies expanding beyond the candy. I added that I thought we could do decorative chocolates to make it artsier, like chocolate high-heeled shoes, and put them for display at some shops around the village. She loved the idea. We talked about getting people to work together where there wasn't as much competition."

Now my eyes teared up. "That's exactly what I was thinking too."

"Great minds think alike," she said.

I turned as I heard a light knock on our front door.

"Can't people read the 'Closed' sign?" Ava barked.

I went to see Chief Tobias standing outside and let him in.

"Hey, why wasn't I invited to the party?" he asked.

I smiled sheepishly. I still was a little miffed at him for putting my grandma in jail.

"I know. I wanted to come and apologize, Jolie. I have to be honest and say I wouldn't have done anything differently, but I do feel awful about what your family went through," he said.

"I know, and thank you for making that effort. I do appreciate it. Would you like some cake?" I asked.

"You know I'm not turning that down. I missed the restaurant being open; I didn't realize how often I come here," he said, slicing a huge slab of cake as I poured him some coffee.

"Yeah, you eat a lot," Ava said.

He grinned at her as he took a huge bite of cake. Everyone laughed.

After he swallowed, he said, "Did you all hear about the property that sold by the park?"

"I saw that," I said.

"Yep, someone is building an Italian restaurant is what I heard, but I don't know who," Teddy said.

"Oh well, Jolie and Betsy will win them over into cross-selling products," Keith said, looking at me and winking.

My face felt like it had turned fifty shades of red.

Ava, who had noticed the exchange, said, "Hey, who bid on you for the date at the auction?" She looked meaningfully at Keith.

"I don't know. I asked my grandma if Aunt Fern or Mom told her and she played coy," I said.

We were interrupted by another knock at the door.

"Man, close down for one week and look what

happens. We may have to stay open twenty-four hours," I said, going to the door.

Detective Meiser was standing there with the most adorable cat ever.

"Who is this?" I cooed as he walked in. The other women got up and gathered around him to get a look at his cat.

"This is Stewart," he said, rubbing the cat's neck; the little white raggedy cat with blackish-gray large spots on him reached up to bite Meiser on his chin. "Hey, we are not doing that again!"

"Again?" I asked.

"That's how we met; I heard that Dr. Libby had adopted out all the animals but this little guy here, so I went to the vet's office today to see him and they had him loose behind the desk. He walked right up to me. I said, 'Hi there, fella,' and he put both paws on my chest and bit me on the chin," he said, grinning at Stewart.

"Ahhh, it's love at first bite," I said, and everyone laughed.

"What happened to his eye?" Ava asked, reaching to pet him. The cat reached to tap her and caught his nail on her top. "Why do cats do this to me?" she whimpered.

"He was abused as a kitten, and they had to remove his eye, but the vet said he was fine. As you can all see, he's ornery as all get out," Meiser said, kissing him on his head. It was nice to see a softer side of him. I could get used to this behavior.

"Did you just come here to show off Stewart?" Keith asked. He didn't seem too thrilled with the attention Meiser was getting. I thought his rudeness was odd.

"No, actually, I came here to see Jolie. What's the best date for you?"

"Huh?" I asked.

"Date? You know, I beat out Keith here at the auction and won a date with you," he said, grinning and rubbing Stewart as Keith fumed.

"Oh snap, girl! Finally, I can get rid of you for a night!" Ava did a "whoop whoop" noise with her fist in the air.

I wasn't so sure this was a good idea.

Grandma Opal's Pineapple Upside Down Cake Recipe

What you will need:

- 1 stick of butter
- 2 ¼ cups packed brown sugar
- Canned sliced pineapples
- Vanilla cake mix
- Cherries

1. Melt one stick of butter in a cast iron skillet.
2. Place 2 ¼ cups packed brown sugar on the bottom of the cast iron skillet.
3. Drain ½ of a 20-ounce can of pineapple juice and put it to the side to add to your cake mix. Add your pineapples on top of the brown sugar.
4. Follow the directions on the vanilla cake mix. (Note: you can also create your vanilla cake mix from scratch.) Add the drained pineapple juice to the batter. Pour the batter on top of the pineapples.
5. Bake at 350 for one hour.
6. Wait 10 to 15 minutes, then flip the cake onto a plate.
7. Add the cherries in the center of the pineapple rings.

Serve and enjoy.

Storage: Cake is best left out and eaten the first

two days after baking. After two days, store in the refrigerator and eat cold or microwave for a few seconds to taste.

NOTE: The secret to the family secret recipe is not listed here—although it was embedded in the story! Go to my website and join my newsletter to find the secret ingredient in the January 2019 issue! Link to the newsletter is below.

Jalapeño Cheddar Cornbread Murder

Book 2 from **The Cast Iron Skillet Mystery Series**

By Jodi Rath

Book Description

Chapter One

My love life has been a full-on roller coaster ride this past year. I prefer not to think about it, let alone talk about it. Summer is here, and I'm ready to chillax poolside; I love living in a state where I get to enjoy each season. It makes me feel like I get a fresh start. Unfortunately, Ava won't let my love life rest.

"I still can't believe the shape your love life is in, girl. How do you manage it?" Ava asked while popping a jalapeño into her mouth.

"It's a gift. Those are HOT!" I exclaimed as her beautiful mocha skin turned into bright red blotches and her eyes bulged out of her head.

"Wa ...WAT ...WATER!!!" she finally managed to spit out, fleeing for the sink.

"No, here, drink this milk instead; it will do more to ease the heat," I said, pouring a glass.

Ava took two big gulps of the eight-ounce glass of milk and began swirling her head left to right in slow motion in a panic.

"More?" I asked.

She nodded her head affirmatively. I wasn't even

able to pour a full glass before she took the carton of milk from me and began chugging it.

"Slow down. You're going to make yourself sick."

"Why is that deathly hot? I love spicy food, but that is ridiculous!" Ava said.

"I'm trying something new in the jalapeño cheddar cornbread recipe."

"Are you trying to kill people by heat index? Good lord, Jolie, did you bother to taste that before using it?" Ava slammed her fist on the counter.

"Why are you crying?" I asked.

"I'm not crying, you fool; the heat from whatever peppers you used is eating through my body and making all the water pour out of my eyes." She reached for a paper towel to blow her nose.

"Calm down. I'm testing it out. I'm not eating them from the jar like a—" I thought better than to finish that statement based on the glare I was getting from Ava. "I'm just saying that I plan to start out using a bit of the juice from the jar and dicing a little up and tasting it in the bread for heat."

"Well, you need to have a death label on those things to warn us spicy lovers ..." Ava stopped midsentence. Her blotchy, red skin was going pale, and she began dry heaving while holding a hand up in a panic. She ran through the swinging doors and I followed in hopes this wouldn't turn into a disaster.

At the front of the restaurant, where the men's and women's bathrooms were, she grabbed the doorknob to the women's and pushed to no avail, her body smacking into the door hard. It looked like it was occupied. At this point, Ava looked like a chipmunk, with cheeks extended and eyes wide.

She looked desperately at the men's room and then didn't hesitate to run into it.

Magda, our new part-time waitress, looked at me shocked. She wasn't used to Ava's antics yet. Last September, our village lost Ellie Siler, my grandma's best friend and one of my favorite women. Magda was recommended to us by Ellie's niece, Betsy, who had taken over her aunt's chocolate store. Ava and I were also able to add two other staff members: Mirabelle, a twenty-four-year-old hostess with the mostess (as Aunt Fern loved to call her) and her sidekick, Spy. Spy was Mirabelle's seeing-eye dog. Mirabelle has Down's syndrome and sight issues. She and Spy were a super duo, greeting each customer as they entered the restaurant.

"I don't understand what I ever saw in you," Bradley said, walking slowly out of the bathroom with some of Ava's barf on him.

She came stomping out after him. "I didn't know you were in there washing your hands. Why didn't you lock the door?"

"Because I just walked in and was planning to be in there for no more than a minute to wash my hands. There aren't many people in here, and none are men. I thought I was safe for a quick minute. I should have known better with you working here, though."

"*Working* here?" Ava scowled.

Oh boy, Bradley had just done himself in. He knew it too. He put his hands up in defense.

"I know, you *co-own* the place—sorry!" he exclaimed.

"Let's take this situation outside please," I said, glancing around at the few customers trying to eat their meals. As Ava and Bradley moved toward the door, I told the patrons I'd be happy to box their meals and that the meals were on the house for the disgusting scene they had just witnessed.

Mirabelle and Spy had been at the restaurant a bit longer than Magda, so I saw Mirabelle grinning as Spy shifted his seated position. The golden retriever looked like he had a grin on his face too.

After some serious groveling and comping the bills, Magda and I worked to clean up the mess as quickly as possible, temporarily closing the restaurant while we did so.

"Miss Jolie, can Spy and I help?" Mirabelle asked as I turned the sign and locked the door for a bit.

A lot of people treated Mirabelle differently. They gawked or felt sorry for her, and acted toward her like she was less in some way. I'm not even sure anyone meant to do it; they didn't seem to understand how to best communicate with her. I used to be the same way until Ava and I took some time over the summer months of high school to coach Special Olympics. We learned how exceptional Mirabelle is at all things.

"Sure thing. Let's see, Magda is cleaning up the men's bathroom and I'm going to do a run-through of the front of the store to make sure everything is clean. I'd like to sweep the floors and wipe down the tables. Which would you like to do?"

"We'll clean tables," Mirabelle exclaimed, and I say exclaimed because every time Mirabelle was given a task, she was fully excited to conquer it. She had energy and a zest for life that I wish I could mimic. Spy did a soft *woof* in agreement as he always seemed to talk to Mirabelle.

We both jumped as we heard a hard knock on our front door.

Bradley's boss, Lou, was standing outside the door. I unlocked and opened the door briefly. "Sorry, Lou, we had an unfortunate incident a few moments ago. I had to close briefly to clean up. I'll open up soon."

"Where is Bradley? He wanted me to meet him here, and here I am. Why we can't talk at the workplace is beyond me. This is ridiculous. He could at least be outside regardless of what 'incident' you've had," he said, making air quotes with his fingers.

"Bradley was part of the incident. He probably ran to change his clothes. I would assume he'll be back soon," I said.

"Figures. I'll call him," he said, grabbing his phone and storming off.

As I went to close and lock up again, Mr. and Mrs. Seevers stormed up to Lou.

"You no good son of a gun; I oughta take that phone and shove it up your—"

"Earl!" Mrs. Seevers exclaimed. "No need for that kind of talk ever, regardless of how much of a creep this guy is."

"What are you two talking about?" Lou demanded.

"We know what you did, and you won't get away with it!" Mr. Seevers seethed.

"You two old bats need to mind your own business. I'm out of here," Lou protested, stomping off with his phone to his ear, probably calling poor Bradley to chew him out.

"Rude," Mirabelle said as I closed and locked the

door again.

"Agreed," I said, wondering what was going on with the Seevers, a typically nice retired couple, and Lou.

About the Author

Moving into her second decade working in education, Jodi Rath has decided to begin a life of crime with The Cast Iron Skillet Mystery Series. Her passion for both mysteries and education led her to combine the two to create her business, MYS ED, where she splits her time between working as an adjunct for Ohio teachers and creating mischief in her fictional writing. She currently resides in a small, cozy village in Ohio with her husband and her eight cats.

Sign up for my monthly newsletter to receive many free pieces of flash fiction, short stories, recipes, and three-minute mysteries that tie into this series at: http://eepurl.com/dIfXdb

Follow me on Facebook at: https://www.facebook.com/jodirathmysed/?modal=admin_todo_tour

Follow my blog at: https://www.jodirath.com/blog

Coming June 21, 2019:

Book 2 in **The Cast Iron Skillet Mystery Series,** titled *Jalapeño Cheddar Cornbread Murder.*

Coming November 15, 2019:
A holiday book in **The Cast Iron Skillet Mystery** Series, titled *Turkey Basted to Death.*

CPSIA information can be obtained
at www.ICGtesting.com
Printed in the USA
LVHW031341231118
598061LV00001B/278/P